SHE, TENACITY

First Printing, 2022

ISBN 9780648557524 (print)
ISBN 9780648557500 (eBook)

She, Tenacity
A *Breakfast Serial* Novel
First published as an email serial.

Cover design by Sarah Bacaller
Other image credits:
Night Skies by Huijun Wang
boy-1300249_1280 by OpenClipart-Vectors on *Pixabay*

To find out more about Sarah's work, visit: www.sarahbacaller.com
Follow Sarah on Instagram @ sarah_bacaller

SHE, TENACITY

SARAH BACALLER

Incisus: Breakfast Serial Projects

Other titles by Sarah:

The Fault Lines Founding Liberty

For articles, book reviews and more, see:
www.sarahbacaller.com/writing

Audiobooks narrated by Sarah include:

Blinky Bill by Dorothy Wall
Seven Little Australians by Ethel Turner
My Brilliant Career by (Stella) Miles Franklin
The Historian's Daughter by Rashida Murphy
A Very Special Gift by Laura Loyola
Australian Christmas Yarns, Vols. I & II, by Mary Grant Bruce
An Introduction to Hegel's Logic by Andy Blunden
Hegel's Philosophy of Mind by G.W.F. Hegel (Trans. W. Wallace)
Rilla of Ingleside by L.M. Montgomery
(Voices of Today full-cast production)

For Cristina
—epitome of feminine agency, tenacity and grit—
And a pro at lounge-room births

xx

For Crystal,
who has had to bear the consequences
of other people's crap, more than most.
The bravest person I know.

And in appreciation of *The Babes Project*,
who support women in situations like Gabrielle's.

How do you build a new life after you've grown up in a crappy home? This is the question I ask myself constantly. What do you use when your hands are empty? When those tasked with your nurture instead tried taking what you didn't even have? I don't know even know what the tools are, let alone how to use them. Nothing comes out of nowhere; someone has to give these things to you, don't they? If not the skills themselves, they have to make a supportive space where you can at least learn to develop them.

I have divested myself of my feelings, my thoughts. Thoughts and feelings are dangerous, too shameful to own. The problem is, the longer you relinquish them, the harder it is to take them back … and then those orphaned feelings and disembodied thoughts become their own force, possessing you beyond your will. But what other choice did I have? This isn't freedom.

I denied ever-present anxieties. I had no-one to hold them for me. I had to divest myself in order to manage. Otherwise, everything would have fallen apart. So I thought. Things were already apart. But to admit those vulnerabilities, those cracks, would have been soft, weak, affected. I couldn't afford that. I couldn't let anything in. In a more functional home, I might have admitted when things were too much. Grown-ups would have held me, told me it was okay … In that moment, I would have trusted *their* ability to manage. I would not have *had* to hold it all together myself. Over time, I would have gained confidence in myself *to* manage.

It never came. My mother could not lead me to belief in myself by believing in me ... maybe because I was not willing to trust *her*. But maybe that unwillingness was well-founded. And now what? Who is there to comfort me? Who is there for me to trust? Who can lead me to trust in myself? And how do I reclaim those orphaned feelings that have taken possession of me? How do I reign them in, harness their potential, become master of myself and merge into one? Must I become my own security? Can I do it myself? Do I need someone else? *Others*?

I do, I have and I have learned how.

Things have changed. I am an adult. And I have choices now. But still I ask, who will lead me to that confidence in the world that comes when another has confidence in me?

Perhaps there *is* one thing you can only find yourself, and perhaps it also comes through others.

CHAPTER 1

May, Year 12

Silhouettes framed by a peachy sky kicked up dust on an autumn horizon. Gab watched, wishing she was bovine so that she could plod her way through life munching grass and flicking flies, like the silhouettes in front of her. She wondered what it would be like to have no conscious thought of herself as a thing, distinct from all other things in the universe. As it was, her mind whirled and whirred and hardly stopped, constantly scrounging for a footing—a footing it never found. Footings were deceptive, anyhow; they crumbled. Gab's footholds couldn't bear her weight when she pushed up. However, she maintained a distinctly even keel on the outside. She had to. She didn't know how *not* to.

The light sank lower as Gab sat on Tony's fence, staring at the sunset. The breeze flicked wisps of auburn hair across her freckled cheeks, across her hazel eyes. Finally, she checked her watch.

"Come on Jack, time to go."

Gab jumped off the fence and then swung her six-year-old brother down too. She was seventeen and family boss—not on paper, but realistically. The family needed someone to hold it together; she had to hold it together, because there was no one to hold *her* if she fell apart.

Gab and Jack ran back to their granny flat on Tony's farm, out on the edge of Wattle Gully. Gab pulled open the flimsy pea-green door with its flywire hanging out, and she and Jack stepped inside.

"Don't traipse dust in here!" came the shrill call of their mother.

Gina was in her usual spot in the throne-room. The sunroom wasn't *really* a throne-room of course, but Gab thought of it like that, in a twisted way. Gina spent her days there from sunrise to sunset—her kingdom. It was her escape and her prison at once. She would sit upon her bed of cushions and faux furs, garbed in flowing floral prints and heavy necklaces. Incense burned, always, on a table to her left and the smell made Gab sick. Images of the gods and gurus of various religious traditions papered the fibro wall behind Gina's throne—Gautama Buddha, Vishnu, Jesus (white, with flowing blonde, distinctly-non-Middle-Eastern hair), Osiris the Egyptian god, Gaia the Mother of Life.

Gina never moved unless she had to. Gab used to wonder why her mother didn't just sleep in that room. But at night, Gina shifted to her musty, fusty bed in its dark, damp corner of the granny flat—a strange contrast to the light, airy sunroom. Occasionally, Gab also wondered whether her mother wanted her and Jack at all. Whenever Gina bothered to engage, there was always admonishment, filtered through a religious saying or proverb—or a complaint with spiritualist spin, disguised in honeyed tones. Gina's faith was an eclectic mix of Gab didn't know what ... but it always seemed to suit Gina's convenience.

Gab knelt down, untying Jack's laces for him.

"Time to get ready for bed, mate," she said, helping him to pull his shoes off. "Go brush your teeth and go toilet. Then I'll read you a story."

"But I don't want to!" Jack whined.

"Come on, Jack," said Gab with a sigh, placing his dusty runners in the old, cracked plastic washing basket by the door. "I don't want to fight. Just do it." She mustered up some energy and enthusiasm. "How about we race? I'll go do teeth and toilet too and we'll see who's finished first ... but make sure you brush your teeth properly! Set your egg timer, okay?"

"Ohhh, okay!" said Jack. Races could generally be counted on to lure him in. "Now say *ready, set, go*!" he instructed.

Gab looked at her watch. "*Ready .... Settttttt ... GO!*" They raced off towards the bathroom, with Jack determined to win and Gab relieved her tactic had worked.

Would Jack settle? If so, Gab could get back to her homework. It was unrelenting this year—Gab's final year of schooling. Unrelenting, exhausting, demanding— something of an escape, but the uncertainty of managing Jack on top of it all made every evening a juggle.

Gab crossed her freckly fingers for good luck while she brushed her teeth, willing the evening to run smoothly.

CHAPTER 2

June, Year 12

Autumn tipped into winter as the days shortened and held their biting chill. Jack spent every short evening riding his bike on the dust patch behind the granny flat, where Tony had helped build a small series of jumps. Jack was one of those kids who had taken to wheels like a duck to water; the chill winter afternoons didn't stop him. Gab had helped him learn to ride a two-wheeler when he was four, but he'd hardly needed any help. He spent hours wheeling around in the dust, and when he came off, it was Gab he called for. He was happy enough out there, and that was helpful because it gave Gab time to study and prepare dinner.

One such afternoon in June, Gab was sitting at the kitchen table finishing up a language analysis for English while nibbling an apple and crackers. The phone rang. The old-school, faded mustard device was sitting on the kitchen table by Gab's elbow. She had already reached out to answer it by the time her mum called out edgily, "Gab? The phone please!" as she always did. Gina hated answering the phone.

"Hello, Gab speaking," answered Gab.

"Hi Gab. It's Mr. Cheng here. I hope I haven't caught you at a bad time?"

"Oh!" Gab's face coloured. "Mr. Cheng ... um, what's up?" She couldn't be in trouble, could she? At lightning speed, she flicked through any possible scenarios that could have precipitated the phone call.

"Nothing bad, Gab; don't worry!" said Mr. Cheng, reading the nervousness in her voice. "When have I ever had to tell you off?"

"Well, you never know?" suggested Gab. Mr. Cheng laughed.

"Actually I've got great news. I thought your mum might like to know that you just scored one hundred percent on today's Maths assessment! That's the second time this year, Gab. Well done!"

"Really?"

"Yeah! Great run. May I speak with your mum?"

"Um, okay, just a minute."

Gab put the receiver down and went to the sunroom. Her mother was sitting cross-legged on the sofa-throne with her eyes closed.

"Mum?" ventured Gab. Gina's eyes snapped open.

"Honey, I'm meditating," she answered.

"Sorry Mum. It's just that Mr. Cheng's on the phone ... He wants to speak with you."

"Why? You in trouble?"

"No."

"Then why's he calling?"

Gab sighed. It wasn't meant to be this hard. "He wants to tell you about my Maths test today. Come on Mum, please." Gina sighed with annoyance and slowly extracted herself from the folds of her seat. She dawdled slowly to the kitchen and picked up the phone.

"Yep?" she said. Gab cringed and walked out of the kitchen. She leaned her head against the wall in the passageway, listening in, while Mr. Cheng told Gina of Gab's impressive result. Gina, however, was not as impressed as he was.

"Okay, that's good, fine," she replied flatly, after he had described Gab's feat. "But maths isn't exactly what you'd call important, is it?" Gab half covered her ears, not wanting to hear, but still nail-bitingly curious. "Yeah, well what about teaching them what's actually going to help them? What about teaching them to pray and seek revelation? Or teaching them about spiritual warfare? Or helping them appreciate the mysteries of the universe, for goodness' sake?" Gina really could get preachy sometimes, Gab thought. She knew that Mr. Cheng would tell Gina that maths was precisely that, a mystery of the universe, a puzzle that humanity had been piecing together for millennia. But Gina obviously wasn't interested.

"Okay, well, thanks for calling then. Bye." And Gina hung up abruptly. "Don't know why he had to bloody call to tell me that," she muttered to herself, but loud enough for Gab to hear. Gab wanted to curl up and die. It was awful. She was slipping off to her room to hide but suddenly turned around.

"Mum," she said in a hushed voice, "Don't you think it's good I did well in my Maths test today?" Her hazel eyes wrestled desperately to hide a look of entreaty, of hunger.

"Yeah, it's great honey," Gina said, as excitedly as if she'd just been informed of the average drying-time for fence paint. "As for your Mr. C, you know my feelings about having someone like *him* in our town. I just wish," and her demeanour suddenly changed in that odd way it was apt to do; she began wringing her hands and seemed close to tears—"I just wish they focused more on teaching you spiritual *truths*, Gabrielle. What *good* is mathematics in guiding you through life? You need insight. You need to hear the voice of revelation, of divine and sacred truths."

Gab hated when her mum talked like this. She hated it, not only because she thought her mum was talking rubbish, but because she simultaneously desired to please Gina. She wanted to believe her mum and to do what made her mum happy. Could she seek 'the voice of revelation' for her mum's sake, even though it frightened the hell out of her?

"Don't worry Mum, it's okay," Gab reassured her mother. "You go and rest in the sunroom. I'll put dinner on."

"You're a good girl, Gabrielle," cooed her mother. "What's for dinner tonight then?" Gina ambled back to her place in the sunroom.

"I'm going to try something new tonight: dal." said Gab. She'd been searching for new recipes. Dal was so cheap to make; plus, you couldn't go wrong with lentils—a protein and vegetable at once.

"What's that?" asked Gina, turning around. "What'd you say?"

"Dal," explained Gab. "It's an Indian dish. Lentils. Like a curry, but I won't make it spicy."

"Cor, Indian? You kidding me?" said her mother. "I don't want that! I want a good, hearty Aussie meal!" It was one of Gina's striking peculiarities that while she was keen to culturally appropriate from whichever religious traditions took her fancy, the everyday, ordinary people who carried on those ancient traditions were treated with disdain—unless they looked and spoke like her. It was as though the religious ideas were completely disconnected from the realities of everyday existence. This jarred with Gab, who—for whatever reasons—was empathetic to a fault.

"You haven't even tried it, Mum. Please, it's really cheap and healthy *and* lentils were on special at work this week."

Gina's eyes filled with tears. "Gabby, don't *do* this to me, honey!" Her breathing rate was increasing, as was her emphasis on each word. "I *really* would just like my usual dinner."

Gab's cheeks reddened, even as she blocked out the shame. Without realising it, gliding into a familiar pattern, Gab bit down and changed tack.

"No worries, Mum. I'll grab some beef for you and Jack." It was okay. She would make dal just for herself. For her mother, she'd get something from the chest freezer out the back; Tony filled it with home-grown beef every year when the steers were sold for market. Gab knew this was what Gina wanted. She'd roast veggies for her mum—and for Jack, because if he saw Gina eating it, he'd want the same.

Gab did everything she could to avoid conflict, because it only made things harder for them all. She felt sorry for her mum; Gina had had such a hard life (and made sure to remind herself and her children of this). Gab pushed down resentment before it even surfaced; before she knew it was there. It seemed the most sensible thing to do—her only real option.

CHAPTER 3

July, Year 12

Gab, Toby, Lauren and Jane were chatting in the study rooms while a wild winter storm raged outdoors. Jane was looking through the VTAC guide, flicking through the results required for any number of courses. It was like roulette: roll the ball, land on a future ...

"*Actuarial* studies? What the hell's *actuarial studies*?" exclaimed Jane, a piece of spinach lodged between her front teeth.

"No idea. Keep going Pop-eye!"

Jane continued, speaking loudly over the whipping wind while digging the spinach out of her teeth: "Bachelor of Agriculture at Melbourne, seventy-two; Biomedicine, ninety-five; Commerce, ninety-three ... ah, got it!" She was victorious over the spinach. "Design, eighty-eight; Economics ... no, wait, that's a Bachelor of Commerce ... Bachelor of Fine Arts in Acting ..." Jane shut the book suddenly. "Why are there so many? I'm never going to be able to choose!" she groaned.

"And why is agriculture low?" asked Gab quietly. "Do they think farmers are stupid?"

"Why does it matter?" asked Jane, eyebrows raised. "Makes it easier to get in. Isn't that what you're putting for first preference?"

"I'm pretty sure it'll be agriculture," said Gab, taking a bite out of a dryish sandwich. "Or maybe something maths related. Or psychology."

"Maths! Geez, you're so weird," Toby exclaimed. "Why??" He ran his hand through his thick black hair, not realising he was depositing large amounts of salt from his hot chips in doing so. He seemed genuinely concerned by Gab's interest in maths.

Gab shrugged. "Each to their own, Tobias. Personally, I can't understand your fascination with luring unsuspecting fish towards fatally sharp hooks so that you can puncture their faces, reel them in and then beat them to death!"

"You're still scarred after the Eyeball Incident of Grade Six camp! Remember that?!" reminisced Toby. "The hook went straight through the flatty's eye! You screamed your head off!" He cackled with a mouthful of hot chips.

"Yeah, well, it was gross!" Gab whacked him with a textbook.

"Toby, you have salt through your hair, you feral. Now, on to more important things than careers and fishing," interjected Lauren, a blonde wisp of a girl with more stamina than most people suspected. "*My* parents are driving down to Melbourne for the weekend. That means *we* have the house to ourselves. Party time or what? Who's in?"

General keenness fluttered round the group. But Gab felt deflated.

"Seriously? Another drinking fest? It's a waste of time and money."

"Touchy, touchy!" chided Lauren. "Everyone's happy to come except you!"

Gab clenched her jaw bitterly. Her classmates were idiots when they were drunk, and she hated being the sober one who cleaned up after them. She had enough cleaning-up to do in life.

"Yeah, Gab," chimed in Jane. "Why won't you come? You always avoid our parties. Isn't Jack at his dad's this weekend?"

Gab couldn't stomach it today.

"Doesn't matter," she murmured. And she shut out the rest of the conversation. She shut out her feelings. She was just like the study room: still, immobile, unwavering despite the intensity of the wind around it. Gab waited and waited, until the moment passed and she could resume life again.

She wasn't willing to mess with the fact that Jack relied on her; that she needed to be on her game for Gina, just in case. She told herself she avoided drinking with her friends because she was mature, because she didn't want to waste a moment of her life in drunken insensibility. The reality was that her options were shaped by her situation, and she couldn't make a decision external to her responsibilities. Besides, she lived a tightly reigned existence. Her reticence to let down her hair was also a fear of being seen, of unravelling. Once she began to relax and let her guard down, who knew what would happen?

The bell rang and the final two periods of the day began. Biology at two o'clock was always a drag. Jane and Lauren sat next to Gab, which wouldn't have bothered her a bit, except that they kept guessing who would and wouldn't come to the party, discussing the whole event without pause. Gab tried to focus instead on writing up the steps from yesterday's plant dissection. She inhabited another world to those girls. Why was she turned off by the things that appealed to everyone else? She wanted to belong but was simultaneously repelled at the thought of joining them. Torn.

Gab met Jack at the school gate like she always did, and they hopped on their bikes. This was how it was—rain, hail or shine, and they were more than used to it. *Lauren couldn't hack doing this*, Gab thought to herself, *as much as I can't hack the idea of that stupid party*. They were just different, that was all. Gab thought perhaps she'd buy the girls some chocolate and chips for the party, even though she wasn't going. That would make up for their argument, or at least show that she wasn't an outsider. She'd drop it off to Lauren's after work tomorrow. Then she'd be back home in time to make dinner for Mum.

Up the final hill before Tony's place, the properties grew bigger. The distance between mailboxes increased with every turn of the pedals. Gab was unlucky enough to ride over a nail halfway up; her front tyre was promptly reduced to a flabby mess.

"Oh damn." She stopped. Jack was up ahead. "Hey Jack! I've got a flat!" she called.

"Oh no!" yelled Jack, "What happened, Gab?" He wheeled around, back to his sister.

Gab squatted by her bike, spinning the wheel to find the culprit.

"There!" Jack pointed to a flat nail head, sunk deep into the rubber. "That's a bad one!"

"We're not far from home," reflected Gab. "You ride on ahead."

"Nah," said Jack, and he walked with Gab instead.

"Got plans for your dad's tomorrow night?" Gab asked after a bit, as they pushed their bikes through the gravel and gum leaves.

"You bet!" exclaimed Jack. "Movie night with popcorn and pizza!"

"Sounds great." Unlike her own father, Jack's dad maintained consistent contact with his son. Gab didn't even know her own father's name.

"What are *you* going to do tomorrow night?" asked Jack.

"Don't know," Gab shrugged.

"You could have a movie night too," Jack suggested.

"With Mum?"

"Yeah, but invite Tony," suggested Jack. "That'll be more fun. Or maybe have one with your mates."

Gab shrugged.

"But you never hang out with them!" Jack argued. "Why? Don't you like them?"

Gab frowned. "Yeah, I do like them! I'm just busy ... with school and work..."

"Who are your friends then?"

"You know! Toby, Lauren, Jane."

"Oh yeah, *those* friends. Is Toby your boyfriend?"

"No!"

"Toby and Gaaaab sitting in a tree..."

Then Gab chased her brother home, but he had the advantage and jumped on his bike, leaving her in a cloud of dust.

CHAPTER 4

The next morning, Gab was up and ready for her nine o'clock Saturday morning shift at the supermarket. As she crouched at the front door putting on her shoes, she suddenly remembered.

"Oh crap, the flat!" she said aloud. "Muuuum!" As soon as her shoes were on, she whizzed to the sunroom, poking her head round the door. "Mum?" she tried again. "May I please borrow your bike? I rode over a nail last night on the way home from school."

No reply. Gina had headphones on. She lifted one side slowly from her ear when she saw Gab.

"What was that, Gabrielle?"

"Your bike, Mum. May I please borrow it? I have a flat and I start work at nine."

Gina frowned. "Why didn't you fix it last night then?" she reproved.

"Oh, I forgot," explained Gab, in her most diplomatic voice. "Sorry."

Gina held out for some time. Then she released an almighty sigh, as though she were making the grandest of sacrifices.

"Fine, fine," she said, finally.

She hadn't ridden her bike in years.

Gab went round and took the bike out of the small shed behind the granny flat. She hosed off the spiderwebs, wiped it down with a towel, grabbed her bag and jumped on. Remaining drips of water on her legs stung as the winter breeze caught them. She was soon speeding down the road, on the trip she'd taken hundreds, if not thousands of times.

* * *

Early afternoon, and Gab was on her way home on her mother's bike. As she turned the corner through the front gate, a scream ripped through the air. *Jack*. Gab's heart dropped, her adrenal glands exploded and she doubled her speed, racing down the long driveway towards him. Awful scenarios raced vividly through her mind until she finally reached him in the dustbowl bike track. He was sitting on the ground, bike tossed aside, arms crossed.

"JACK! Jack! You okay?" she cried, throwing down her mum's bike without a second glance and racing over to him. "What's up?"

"I CAN'T DO IT!" he yelled. "I CAN'T DO A MONO!"

"Are you okay?"

"No! Because I can't do a mono!!"

Gab was so relieved she tipped back and lay in the dust. Jack gave a frustrated squeal and kicked his feet. Gab rubbed his back.

"Don't worry mate, you'll get there."

"NO. I. WON'T!" he yelled. He was hot and flustered after hours of riding.

"Just keep at it."

"NO NO NO! I hate that stupid bike!"

"Time to do something different," said Gab calmingly.

"NO! I WANT TO DO A MONO!" Jack was not in a good space.

"You look hot, kiddo," said Gab, trying hard to keep her voice even. "How about you come in and I make you a giant cold Milo?"

"With a scoop of ice-cream?"

"Yep!"

Now *that* was what Jack wanted to hear.

"Oh yeah!! Please Gab! The biggest one you ever made!"

Gab stood up and pulled her brother up with her. She was relieved. Her temper had been rising along with his, and she feared not being able to subdue it. Jack didn't always flip so easily from mighty tantrum to happy agreement.

"Come on, mate. Not long 'til your dad arrives."

CHAPTER 5

On Sunday it rained all day. Gab spent the day studying in her room, with a few stolen hours of leisurely reading in the afternoon. The water pooled on the dust outside, so devoid of moisture that it was hydrophobic; then slowly, slowly, slowly, gravity did its work and the seeping-in began. It hadn't eased off by evening when Brian dropped Jack home. Gab put Jack straight in the bath before putting him to bed with a story.

By next morning, the rain had stopped. Gab was up early to fix her bike before Gina had even stirred. Porridge for breakfast for Jack and herself, lunch made and packed for them both—and still time to fix her bike with the puncture kit that sat in the bottom drawer of her dresser.

Gab worked outside in the fresh morning light, as the sun danced through the maze of eucalypts along the property's edge. The birds sang their morning songs and the occasional bovine *moo* cut an awkward contrast to the dainty twittering of blackbirds and the melodic hymns of the currawongs. Gab had fixed plenty of punctures before, and she had the tyre patched up and pumped without a hitch. She and Jack headed off as Gina was just waking up.

Gab's first interaction with her mother that day was hearing her name shrilly called as she pulled open the front door that afternoon.

"GABRIELLE!"

Gab didn't answer immediately. She put down her bag, took off her shoes and walked quietly to the sunroom, her socks sliding along the linoleum.

"Hi Mum. What's up?"

"Gabrielle!" said her mum melodramatically. "*Where* did you leave my bicycle on Saturday after you borrowed it?"

Gab thought back and frowned. What had she been doing again? Oh, yes—Jack's scream, racing to him, wrangling him with visions of cold milo.

"I guess … I probably left it out the back. I went to check on Jack because he was screaming."

"Don't justify yourself! Tell me what you did then?"

"I came inside and cooked dinner."

"And the bike?"

Gab looked sheepish. "I guess I left it out there. Sorry Mum."

"And what happened yesterday?"

"I studied … and … it rained a lot." Gab could see where this was going.

Gina had a pained look. "It's alright Gab. I … forgive you."

The words came out with effort that sounded almost feigned. "Just … don't do it again. Remember, that bike was a special gift for my thirtieth birthday. You treat it like junk! That's not the way you should treat other people's things!"

"Mum…" Gab swallowed down the sick feeling rising in her throat, "you don't even ride that bike."

Gina's eyes snapped open quickly.

"That's *not* the point Gabrielle," she said, her voice hard. "It's the *principle* of the thing. If you borrow something, put it back. Don't leave it out to get ruined!"

"But Jack was upset. I was just seeing if …"

"Enough! No excuses. Now, I need some quiet. I'm practicing a new healing mantra. I've had terrible stiffness in my wrists this week. I can hardly move them."

"I'll go and put it away, Mum."

"Good!"

Gab turned around, pushed it all from her mind and went to put the bike away. She was looking forward to her homework.

CHAPTER 6

On Thursday morning, Gab rose and was surprised to find Gina up and awake, sitting on her throne. It really was quite a beautiful spot in the morning light, Gab thought, and a pity that the room had become so claustrophobic, with its dramatic imagery, the smell of incense and the years of worries, confusions, excuses and illusions that swam in there.

Gab and Jack got ready for school, and Gab went to grab her bike from the back shed. But it wasn't there. That was odd, because it was always there.

"Jack," she yelled to her brother, who was just coming down the front steps. "Have you seen my bike?"

"Shed!" Jack yelled back.

"Nah, it's not there!" Gab called. She needed that bike for getting to school on time. She had a test that morning in her first period of biology; she could not afford to be late. Gab thought back to the last place she'd had it—same as always, she'd put it in the shed after coming home from school last night. But it definitely wasn't there. Maybe it had been stolen?

Gab raced around to the side of the house where an old fence made a narrow passage against the wall and long grass grew—a haven for snakes. She stepped gingerly through but couldn't see it there. Where was it?

Done with the long grass, Gab ran to the edge of the closest paddock and climbed on the fence to get a wide view of it. Dew laced the grass and had solidified into frost in round patches. It looked magical, but Gab was too agitated to appreciate it. The bike did not appear to be in the paddock and there were no tracks. So she jumped off the fence and jogged up the long driveway and around the turn, with increasing panic, hoping to see her bike on the gravel. But it wasn't there. The clock was ticking. Maybe Mum would let her borrow *her* bike again ... But she really didn't want to have to ask.

Up to the road and back down the driveway again. Nearer to the road lay smaller paddock, lined with trees. In it sat a skip bin. Gab had a sick feeling when she looked at that bin. She'd been avoiding it, but she had looked everywhere else now. She ran towards it. She was about to jump up and look in when she noticed the rim of a tyre peering out from behind the skip. It was her front tyre. The bike was there.

"AHHHH!" cried Gab, with deep relief.

Jack rode up the drive, ready to be on his way to school.

"What's your bike doing there, Gab?" he called, pulling up against the fence.

"No idea!" replied Gab. "You didn't put it here, did you?"

"Nah, no way," he said. "I wouldn't do that."

"Are you sure?" she asked, even though she knew he wouldn't.

"Yeah, promise!"

"How'd it get here?!" For a moment, Gab questioned her sanity and her memory. Had she left it in this spot for some reason? But she hadn't been near the skip last night. Maybe she was finally cracking. That thought was a lightning rod of pain that landed somewhere in her guts, but she pushed it aside. She was *sure* she hadn't left her bike by the skip. Wasn't she?

That biology test was looming. It was time to think of other things. Gab jumped on her bike and she and Jack rode to school.

After the test however, the mystery of the bike stirred in the back of her mind again and plagued her for the rest of the day. Had someone come down the property and taken her bike out of the shed? Was it some kind of odd revenge? A prank? Surely Lauren or Jane wouldn't ... But then, Gab always locked the shed at night. And the lock hadn't been broken when she'd checked that morning ... unless ...

When Gab arrived home that afternoon, she walked to the sunroom.

"Mum, my bike was out in the paddock this morning, hidden behind the skip," she said.

"Was it?" said Gina, shrugging. "That's odd." Gab tried hard to detect any note of sarcasm in her mother's voice; Gina was too hard to read.

"Yeah, it is weird," agreed Gab. "Took me ages to find it and I was nearly late!"

Gina's eyes flicked open.

"Do you ... have any idea how it got there?" Gab continued. "I put it away in the shed yesterday, like always."

"I have one word for you Gabrielle," said Gina, fixing her gaze on Gab. "Karma."

"What do you mean, Mum?" Gab asked quietly, her heart sinking. She had wondered about this but hadn't wanted to believe it.

"You left *my* bike out in the rain." said Gina, by way of explanation.

"So ..."

"So I left yours out," said Gina, as she lay her head back on the couch and pulled on a sleep mask. "Karma."

"But Mum! It was an accident! Jack was screaming!"

"Oh, come on Gabrielle."

"I had a Biology SAC this morning!"

Gina was silent. Gab felt like she was a volcano with lava rising, rising, rising to eruption point ... she clenched her jaw, her fists, her back ...

But just as she was about to explode ... pfffffff. It was gone. She was numb and floating somewhere in the very heights of her skull. She walked quickly to the bathroom. As she went in, her feelings surged suddenly and she SLAMMED the door as hard as she could. The walls rattled and the soap fell off its shelf in the shower. Gab ran the bath, undressed, and submerged herself under the water time after time after time. She wanted to forget it all. Breathing was such an inconvenience.

CHAPTER 7

August, Year 12

Winter was moving towards spring. The midyear holidays passed and there was a growing tightness in Gab's chest, which she attributed to the rapidly approaching exams. Those moments between being asleep and awake—moments Gab used to enjoy—were no longer a refuge, as each day the weight of life fell upon her again. But she told herself she could handle it. She *was* handling it. What choice did she have?

The wind bit their faces and their fingers as Gab and Jack whizzed down the road to school on a Monday morning in August. Gab farewelled Jack at his gate and then walked through hers. She pulled off her helmet, locked her bike in the school bike shed and headed into the study room with its lingering, mingling smells of teenage sweat, cheap deodorant and overripe bananas. She sat at her desk, shoving her bag underneath and grabbing out her Maths books. She had fifteen minutes to finish off the bonus homework questions before other students would start arriving. Concentrating was impossible once they did, especially with plans for the Year 12 formal well under way—a job in the hands of the Year Twelves themselves. It was all about colour theme at the moment—teal and black, teal and silver, pink and grey, or gold and black ... this was the big question. Gab didn't really care, but it was hard to concentrate on homework when

Jen, Lauren and Mika were yelling at Jane and Candice about why teal with silver was so much better than teal with black. Inevitably, the bell would ring and they'd be no nearer deciding the colour scheme than they had been three weeks before.

Mr. Cheng stood before the Year 12 Maths class of six students and demonstrated patiently, for the hundredth time, how to find the gradient of an asymptote. Gab had got it the first time, months ago, so she raced ahead, working through the day's revision exercises. She liked maths because of its predictability. There were logical steps that led to logical answers, and those answers were always clear: they were either right or wrong. There was no grey. The trick was simply finding where you'd gone wrong, if you had. Gab threw herself into her work and lost herself there. She forgot about the tightness in her chest, always pleased for the opportunity to test out what she'd learned. In that sense, exams wouldn't be so bad. Only, she didn't want to think about what would happen afterwards.

Gab was the last to leave the classroom. She wanted to finish so there wouldn't be any homework that night. Mr. Cheng was packing up slowly, conscious of Gab's presence, giving her time.

"Done!" Gab put her pen down and looked up at Mr. Cheng. "Sorry Mr. C. Didn't mean to hold you up!"

"No, no, you didn't," he said graciously, even though she had.

Gab hastily gathered her belongings. They exited the classroom together.

"How's Jack?" Mr. C. asked, as they walked down the corridor and then out into the schoolyard.

"He's okay," said Gab, enjoying the almost-spring sunshine on her face. "But getting him to do his readers at night is impossible! It's a nightmare."

"Keep at it," encouraged Mr. Cheng. "He'll take to it in his own time."

"It gets exhausting," Gab confessed. "I try to keep it fun, though."

"Sounds like you're right on track," said Mr. C. "It's not easy, hey?"

"I'll say," agreed Gab. They were nearing the Year 12 study block.

"Gab, the deadline for uni preferences is coming up." Mr. Cheng had been curious about this for a while. "Have you decided on your preferences?" He'd been watching Gab's progress for years and wanted her to succeed. She was hardworking.

"I'm not sure," answered Gab, putting her books down on the study block deck and jumped up to sit on the railings. "But I think I want to study agriculture in Melbourne."

"Awesome!" her teacher replied with enthusiasm. "That sounds just right. But you'll succeed at anything you put your mind to. You're determined and focused." If he was tentative about particular external obstacles in her way, he didn't show it.

"Thanks," Gab said, colouring. "I'm also thinking about psychology or data science."

"They're good options too," said Mr. C. "They suit your interests and skills. You'll get your first preference. I don't doubt it."

"Don't get your hopes up Mr. C … or mine!" joked Gab, half seriously.

"I think we're pretty safe on that one!" said Mr. C, waving and walking off towards the staff room. "I'd bet on it … and I'm not a betting man!"

Gab smiled, both resisting and relishing the confidence he placed in her. She'd known Mr. C. since primary school. He'd been her Grade 6 teacher before he began teaching at the secondary school. In a small town, they needed local teachers to fill gaps and Mr. C. was the best Maths teacher going around. When Mr. Gosford had retired after teaching for thirty years, it was Mr. Cheng who stepped into the senior Maths teaching role.

Gab was walking through the study room door when she heard her name called from outside.

CHAPTER 8

"Gab! Gab!"

It was Tess, a lonely Year 8 girl. Tess stood by the library doors every lunchtime, until Mrs. Millbush, the librarian, had eaten her lunch and opened the library to students. Gab always made sure to say hello when she saw her. Tess adored Gab, and while her zealous hugs were sometimes more than Gab wanted, Gab let that slide, knowing that Tess craved positive attention.

Gab put her books down on the study room veranda for the second time in ten minutes walked towards Tess. The younger girl threw her arms around Gab and squeezed. She smelled faintly of cheddar cheese and cats, and wore an ankle-length skirt, a plaid shirt, and her hair in a long ponytail.

"How are you, Tess?" asked Gab.

"I'm okaaay," Tess replied, finishing her hug reluctantly and standing right up close to Gab, a bit closer than was socially acceptable. "It's sooo hot though." Unfortunately Tess complained a lot, so other kids avoided her. Gab often thought that if Tess's peers had taken time to understand Tess's challenges, they'd have more time for her.

"I got 49% on a math test today," Tess whined, "but I *should* have gotten higher. It's not *fair*. Mrs. O'Grady's always giving me low marks in Maths!"

"Oh, that's okay," said Gab, "you'll do better next time. Maybe I could help you study?"

"What if I *don't* do better next time?" worried Tess. "My dad says if I fail another test, I'm banned from TV for a week! I'll miss all my favourite shows. I can't let that happen!"

"Come on," said Gab, "let's go to the canteen."

The school canteen was a little tin shack under a flowering gum. It sat on the back fence of the school, with cords running out from one of the portable classrooms to power its mini fridge and freezer. The latter was always stocked abundantly with icy-poles, but even then they were never enough for the voracious student appetite for cooling treats.

"What are you going to buy?" asked Tess suggestively as they approached the canteen-shed.

"An icy-pole for you. Want one?"

"Yay! Yes please! You're so nice." Tess hugged Gab mid-stroll. "You're always getting me icy poles!"

And it was true. But what had started as a thoughtful deed had now led to a situation where Tess would now come looking for Gab, suggestively hedging for treats without actually asking directly. And Gab hated to say no. She figured it was worth giving in, even if she did feel a little harried at times; worn down even. But she wasn't about to hurt the feelings of an already fragile and lonely thirteen-year-old, just to save fifty cents and ten minutes of her time. Nevertheless, if she offered first, she wouldn't be nagged.

Having made their purchase, Gab walked Tess back to the library.

"What are you going to do for the rest of lunchtime?" Gab asked.

"I don't know. Can you come and hang out with me in the library? Can we play chess?" Tess asked.

"Oh, not today, Tess. I came out of Maths late and I haven't had lunch yet."

"Awww," Tess whined.

"Another time," assured Gab.

"Okay," said Tess. "I'll probably just play computer games then or talk to Mrs. Milbush. At least I'll have this icy pole while I'm waiting for the library to open."

They reached the library and Gab said good-bye, but Tess wouldn't let her leave without a third hug.

Back at the study block veranda, Gab picked up the books from where she'd left them and headed inside to finish her icy pole and have her lunch.

CHAPTER 9

August, Year 12

Tony knocked on the door early one Sunday morning and Gab opened up.

"Hey, Tony!" she said.

"Hey Gabby," he greeted her jovially. "I'm heading down to the creek to do some planting. Want to join me? Figured you might need a break from all that study!"

"Oh yeah, sure!" said Gab, pleased. She liked helping Tony on the farm. Gina and Gab had moved into Tony's granny flat when Gab was six weeks old and had been there ever since. Tony and Gina had been at school together—the same high school Gab was at now—and their mothers had been best friends. When Gab was little, she used to imagine Tony proposing to her mum. She had been captivated by the idea of them getting married and would fantasise about it in bed at night to help her get to sleep, though she never in a million years would have told anyone. With a couple more years up her sleeve now though, Gab realised that that just wasn't the relationship the two of them had. Tony was doing a favour for a long-time peer whom he felt empathy for and, in a sense, was paying homage to his generous mother and her friendships. Gab wasn't even sure she'd call her mum and Tony friends, though they were in a way. But it was hard for anyone to enjoy Gina's company when she was so unpredictable, so moody.

Tony did a good job of looking out for them, like filling up the chest freezer with beef every year. So, Gab was glad to be able to help Tony on the property when she could, and he enjoyed her company. She was a smart and helpful kid, he thought, who found herself in tough circumstances and needed to cop a break sometimes. Every year since she'd been eight, Tony sold Gab a young steer at a price appropriate to her budget. When the steers went to market, she'd make a decent profit from her fattened beast. Tony would always deliver the cash with a grin, talking with Gab about current market prices and the outlook for the coming year.

They lived on challenging and beautiful country with unpredictable rains and long dry patches in between. The more moisture they could store in the soil, the better. Moisture meant increased biodiversity, greater health. Healthier soil meant more nutritious grass, and more nutritious grass mean happier, healthier steers. Vegetation also lowered surface temperatures; but they had to think carefully about the locations of planting and the choices of plants, because bushfires were a very real threat too.

This year, Gab had been studying sustainable land management in her agriculture unit at school, and she had been filling Tony in on everything she'd learned. He took on her advice and enjoyed discussing land management strategies with her. With a ute-load of local native plants recently sourced, today they were going to begin revegetating the creek-bed to prevent further erosion.

"Tony?" asked Gab, with a sudden flash of curiosity as the two of them unloaded their tools from the ute, "when did you buy this farm?" They were getting ready to dig holes for the new plants along the creek-bed.

"Ah! Well, a long time ago now," said Tony, leaned on his shovel. "How old are you, love?"

"Seventeen."

"You and your mum moved into the granny flat when you were only a few weeks old. Feels like yesterday. You were a tiny little thing, with big bright eyes. I'd been here two years then. So I guess that makes it nineteen years since I bought the place."

"Oh! I always thought you'd grown up here!"

"Me? Nah. My parents ran the post office in town." He resumed digging.

"Ha, really?"

"Yeah. We lived above the shop. Then, I moved to Sydney when I was eighteen. Needed a change."

"That's a long way away."

"Yeah, was a long way—but that was what I wanted. Travelled by train. Decided to study accounting at uni of all things. My dad had been a doctor before taking on the post office and made sure I did well in school. He'd moved here from Melbourne looking for a change of pace, but I'm not sure he found it!"

"So did you work in Sydney after you finished uni?"

"Yeah, I worked at an accounting firm for a couple of years."

"Did you like it?"

"Well, I learned a lot. I could find my way around the city. Met some interesting folk. I also watched how the business was run and learned that it's better to own up to your mistakes then hide 'em."

"Did *you* make mistakes?" Gab got on her knees and began taking plants out of their black plastic pots and teasing out the roots.

Tony laughed. "Oh yeah, plenty. The client is always right, Gab, even when they're not!" He paused. "I kinda missed being out here though. The space. The stars. The trees."

"So you bought this property and moved back to Wattle Gully?" Gab smoothed the soil around the chocolate lilies she'd just planted.

"Well, I put a deposit down on it. I'd been talking to a mate in town, Jim Stafford; you know him? He makes those iron junk sculptures."

"Oh yeah, I know him."

"Well, Jim's a mate of mine from school and he told me about this property when it came up for sale. It was perfect see, because of the granny flat. My mum and dad were getting too old to run the post office, so they came to live in it while I lived in the main house." Tony put down his shovel and came to join Gab with the planting.

"But what happened to them? They can't have been here long before we came."

"Yeah, true. After they'd been here with me for about a year, my sister Amanda invited them to go down and live with her. She's down south on the Mornington Peninsula."

"And they went?" Gab asked.

"Well," explained Tony, "my dad's health was going downhill, and he needed to be close to specialists."

"But what about you?" asked Gab.

"Oh well, it was okay. I made a commitment here and wanted to stick it out, for a minimum of five years."

"And you're still here."

"Yep, I'm still here. And look at the good we're doin'!" Tony motioned to the plants they'd put in while chatting. "Plus," he added, "It meant I could offer the granny flat to you and your mum."

"Tony ..." suddenly, Gab wanted to ask him something important; something that her mother had always reprimanded her for asking about; something Gab thought she had always been too shy to ask Tony.

"Tony ... do you know anything about my dad?"

Tony paused and looked at her. He wiped his brow with his forearm, leaving a smear of dirt across his head.

"I can't say I do, love."

"Oh," said Gab.

"I'm sorry." He really meant it.

"It's okay. I shouldn't have asked," Gab apologised. But Tony frowned.

"Now then, what makes you say that? Course you're allowed to ask!"

Gab shrugged, feeling dumb, staring blankly at the bobbing flower-heads in front of her.

"Has your mum told you anything?" Tony asked. "Anything at all?"

Gab looked up at him and smiled a little; he looked comical with his unperceived dirt smear.

"Nope," answered Gab. "You've got some dirt, Tony ... just ... there."

"Oh yeah, I know," he winked. "I meant for that to happen." Gab grinned. But her smile faded again.

"You know, when I ask Mum, she gets really upset at me ... just for being curious."

"That's too bad, love. It's natural to want to know." Tony thought back to when Gab was a child, how she'd pepper him with questions. She had no recollection now of having asked him those questions; she thought it was the first time. But it wasn't and he remembered.

"So, you don't know who he was?" she concluded.

"No, I don't. There were plenty of rumours going round after you were born, of course, but they weren't worth listening to. I figured the best thing to do was just shut up and be useful. Things were what they were. Telling stories about it wasn't going to help your mum—or you."

"Sometimes I don't think about him for ages, Tony. My ... dad... I mean." The title felt awkward for someone who had never been there. "But then sometimes, I want to know so badly. It's like a hole inside me that's pulling the rest of me down into it. I want to know who I am."

"Oh, families are complicated," sighed Tony. He didn't know what else to say.

Suddenly Gab spotted something.

"Hey, Tony! Tony! Look!" Gab ran over to where she had seen small movements under a manna gum and Tony followed, navigating carefully around their newly situated plants. Gab bent over with her hands on her knees.

"I think the baby's still alive!" said Gab, looking closely at a fallen possum, which must have perished only hours earlier. A tiny wriggly face peeped out of its dead mother's pouch.

"Ohhh, bless," said Tony, always a sucker for little creatures with big eyes. Gab pulled off her jumper and gradually wedged it under the dead mother possum.

"Come on, little guy," she urged, gently nudging the baby up and out of the pouch. "You must be pretty thirsty by now."

Tony and Gab had nursed a few injured creatures in their time, but it had been a while since they'd found an orphaned possum.

"You got a dropper at your place, Gab? You want to take the baby back to the granny flat, or you want me to take it to my place?" Tony asked.

"I'll take the little guy," said Gab, peering at the little pink and grey creature. It was bereft of its mother and her heart hurt for it.

"He'll need to drink during the day while you're at school though," Tony pointed out.

"You want to possum-sit while I'm there?"

"Yeah, alright. Then you come collect him from me in the evenings and keep him overnight."

"Sounds like a good custody arrangement," Gab said, and they laughed.

Jimbo the Possum (as they christened it) grew to its adult size, nourished under their care. During late October, Tony built a new possum box and lodged it in one of the manna gums under which they had found it. That was where they released Jimbo, who was not afraid of them and was often seen clambering along the guttering of Tony's veranda, stopping in long enough for Tony to give him some apple.

CHAPTER 10

Early November, Year 12

Exam time came. Gab had studied consistently and intently, as always. In the preceding weeks, she had felt extraordinarily eager to do her best and knew that she was ready, tight-chestedness notwithstanding. But on the morning of her first exam—Maths—her nervousness was overwhelming.

She stared shakily into cereal she couldn't eat. Finally, she forced down three mouthfuls even though it was like swallowing cardboard.

Gab helped Jack to get ready for school; they packed their bags and then went out to grab their bikes. Gab had double checked that hers was in the shed the night before.

The ride to school stopped Gab from shaking, but she started again after she'd dumped her bag in the study block and was walking towards the exam rooms.

The small class of students gathered in twos and threes around the building. Some of them were loud and jovial, most were hushed and tense. The doors were set to open in five minutes when Mr. Cheng walked over.

"Hey everyone!" he smiled, as he approached. The students waved, trying to smile, calling out greetings.

"I just wanted to wish you all good luck," Mr. C. said. "Actually, you don't need good luck. You've worked hard and it'll pay off. Just go and do your thing."

He went round and spoke a few encouraging words to each of his students, asking them how they were, telling them they'd be fine. When he came to Gab, he didn't say much—only four words, but they were imbued with confidence:

"Go for it, kiddo."

Gab smiled, despite the tornado riling in her stomach.

Maths, more Maths, Biology, English, Agriculture and Psychology. One by one, Gab ticked them off as the exams fell like dominoes at the end of a long and winding year.

And at the end of them, she felt strangely bereft. School had structured her life since ... well, always. It had given her a place, a routine, goals for the future. It had placed her in a community that was generally supportive, stable—and had mitigated the turbulence at home. That wasn't to say it had always been easy, or that the usual social dramas didn't occur. They did. But they were less troubling, less dramatic, than life at home. Gab, Jane, Lauren, Toby ... the whole of the year level ... had been together since primary school. They knew each other too well. Many were ready for a change of scene, and admittedly, Gab found none of her friendships particularly compelling, though she and Toby had enjoyed a healthy rivalry.

Gab had never had friends over to her house. Once, in Grade 1, a girl named Sally had come over. But Sally had seen a rat in the kitchen and screamed and wanted to go home. And then she'd told her mother about it and her mother forbade her to go back. That was the last time Gab made the mistake of inviting people in. She wouldn't risk such humiliation again and necessarily kept other kids at a distance.

Year 12 celebrations came and went. Tess cried on Gab's last day and hugged her for longer than ever, and Gab promised to keep in touch. Muck up day and the Year 12 formal (Gab partnered up with Toby, as much for convenience as anything) were followed by the tense wait, mingled with summer liberation, in the lead up to the release of results.

As Mr. Cheng had suspected, Gab topped her Maths class; she also topped her Biology and Agriculture Studies classes. Her final score was outdone by only one other student, and the two of them still gained the highest scores ever attained by students at their regional high school.

The Year 12 teachers were thoroughly proud and wholeheartedly bestowed their students with awards and praise at school presentation night—which Gina didn't attend. But Tony went along and spoke with Mr. Cheng afterwards about Gab's success, the possibilities for her upcoming year, and the shame it was that Gina just didn't seem interested. "A bloody shame, that's what it is. Bloody disgraceful," was the way Tony described it. Mr. Cheng didn't use the same words—not at presentation night anyhow—but he was in agreement with Tony. "If only there was more we could do," said Tony, even though he already did a lot. And Mr. Cheng agreed, but unfortunately the one thing they couldn't change was Gina—and the responsibility that came with her and fell upon Gab. The conversation only strengthened their resolve to do what they could for Gab, when they could.

Gab didn't know anything about this, of course; she would have felt mortified and defensive of her mother. The awards night had been a real triumph for her, in recognition of her hard work and outstanding results. She only allowed herself to feel sorry for her poor mother, who found life so difficult that she didn't want to leave the house—even for her daughter's Year 12 presentation night. And what else could Gab do? What else was there to feel? Gab couldn't trade families. She couldn't yell at her mother or vent her disappointment without throwing her mother into spirals of violent lament. She couldn't change what had happened. So, she allowed it to silently shape her, and she contorted herself to fit around the poky circumstances of the situation, like she always did—perhaps to her own detriment, but also for her own survival.

CHAPTER 11

School was over. All Gab's peers were abuzz with their plans for the next year, but Gab mostly avoided those conversations and tried not to think about it too much. She spent her days reading, working at the supermarket, traipsing around the farm and potting up seedlings to plant out with Tony.

And so, Christmas and New Year came and went without much fuss. Tony had Gina, Gab and Jack around for Christmas lunch and didn't let Gab cook a thing, even though she offered again and again in the lead up. Tony was handy in the kitchen, and in the end, Gab relished the opportunity to sit back and relax while he filled the table with almost more food than it could bear, and certainly more than they could eat in one sitting. She did manage to help with the washing up afterwards, however.

Around the Christmas table, they pulled on crackers and put on paper crowns—even Gina—and they laughed at stupid Christmas jokes and concocted better ones. Tony gave Jack a new bike for Christmas, which was a massive surprise for them all. To Gina, he gave a department store gift card, imagining she could buy some new bedding or crockery for the granny flat. And to Gab, he gave a voucher for year-long subscription to *Regenerative Farming* magazine.

And what did Tony receive? Well, with her supermarket income, Gab had been saving up for a metal-junk sculpture of a cow for

Tony, which also functioned as a new mailbox. It was made by Jim Stafford, Tony's old school mate. Tony was delighted and beamed with pleasure. Gina gave him a couple of pairs of socks (which he did genuinely need) and Jack gave him another sculpture, home-made, of small timber offcuts glued and hammered together. Christmas lunch at Tony's was one happy family memory that Gab did hold, even if Gina could never afford to give her anything much. Gina reasoned to herself that Gab had her own money, so she wasn't really missing out.

I've got my work money, Gab told herself, in a strange parallel to Gina's reasoning, *so it's no big deal that Mum doesn't give me much.* And she really believed it.

Christmas lunch formalities (informal as they were) usually ended when Brian, Jack's dad, came up and honked his car horn, indicating that it was time for Jack to grab his things and go to his dad's for the night. This was great for Jack—it was Christmas round two, and his dad always gave great presents, although he was so delighted with the bike that he could barely imagine more. For a seven-year-old kid, that was saying something.

Jack said bye to Tony, Gina and Gab, and ran out with his bag to his dad's ute, only to come pelting back in again, out of breath.

"Hey Gab, this is for you from Dad! See ya!" And Jack practically threw a small package and a card at Gab, so eager was he to be off on his next Christmas adventure.

"Hey, thanks!" said Gab. "Say thanks to your dad for me, Jack!" she yelled after him.

"I will!" came the voice, trailing off as the car door slammed shut.

Gab looked down at the parcel in her hands. She opened the card.

Dear Gab,

Congratulations on finishing school. Merry Christmas and happy 18th for January 5th too.

This is to say thanks for looking after Jack.

From, Brian.

Awww, thought Gab, but didn't say it aloud. It felt more good to be recognised.

"What's that?" asked Gina suspiciously. "What did Brian give you?"

"Nothing Mum, just a Christmas card," said Gab, hiding the card and gift under the table.

"Oh!" said Gina to Tony, "looks like *Gab*'s getting gifts from Brian now. What about *me*? Can't remember the last time he gave *me* a gift!"

"Give her a break, Jeen," said Tony, taking a swig of beer. But Gina's misplaced indignation couldn't take away from the pleasure Gab felt when she surreptitiously opened the package and found a fine gold necklace, with a round pendant stamped 'G'. She quickly tucked it back into its box and slipped it into her pocket.

Gab, Gina and Tony spent the rest of the afternoon chatting, snoozing, drinking (Gina and Tony) and reading (Gab).

As Gab went to bed that night, she concluded that it had been a pretty good Christmas.

CHAPTER 12

January

Gab turned eighteen in early January but didn't have a party, nor did she tell anyone. Tony knew though. It was the morning of her birthday and she'd been making pancakes and bacon when he knocked on the door. She opened it up. He greeted her with a grin and handed her an envelope.

"Happy birthday, Gabby!"

"Thanks Tony," Gab grinned.

"You're an adult now. But then, you've always been one, haven't you?"

Gab shrugged as she peeled open the envelope and pulled out a card with a highland cow on the front. Inside, Tony had written,

Dear Gabby,

Wishing you a very happy birthday. Here's some money to go and get your L plates, and some extra cash for a couple of driving lessons.

Cheers, Tony.

"Oh wow, Tony! Thanks!"

It was Tony who had taught Gab how to drive really, out in the paddock in his old Commodore. Gab was fine at driving round the paddock, but she hadn't gone out onto the roads yet. While the other kids her age had gotten their provisional licences one by one over the last twelve months, she hadn't even gone for her learner's permit.

"Once you get your L plates," said Tony cheerfully, "you can be my chauffeur in the ute. You'll need to clock up a whole bunch of hours, so maybe we can do some driving together."

"Oh! That'd be awesome, Tony!" said Gab. She'd felt stuck when it came to getting her licence. As Gina didn't have a car, nor the temperament for teaching in a calm and careful manner, Gab had pushed the whole operation aside. She hadn't wanted to bother Tony about it and had other things to focus on. Besides, she was used to riding her bike everywhere.

"Hey Tony, want to come in and have pancakes?"

He was still standing on the doorstep.

"Oh, you sure, love? Okay, thanks!"

So, Tony came in and Gab boiled the kettle for tea. Tony popped his head into Gina's sunroom on the way to the kitchen, as the eastern rays danced with morning freshness on the crusty wall of deities.

"Hey Gina," he said. "Your little girl's turning 18 today, hey?"

Gina was sitting cross-legged on her couch, reading the Bhagavad Gita. The smell of incense clashed with the spacious morning air that had come in when Tony entered the house.

"What's age, Tony? It is but an illusion. Who knows how long our souls have truly been on this earth?"

Tony bristled. "C'mon Gina, it's a big day for her. What did you get her for her birthday?"

Gina looked up at Tony.

"You know my financial situation, Tony," she said, clenching her teeth. Then her eyebrows rose, her body slumped and her eyes implored. "I know what you're thinking, okay? But you don't know how hard it is!" Gina was ever the victim of fortune. "I *am* getting her take-away for dinner tonight, you know!" she whined. "That's something, isn't it? I couldn't afford anything else!"

Tony was ready to explode as Gab called out, "Tea's ready, Tony!" He didn't want to ruin her morning, so he held his tongue. He would turn his utter indignation into a resolve to celebrate with Gab as heartily as he could.

Tony sat down at the table. There was a picture from Jack for his sister, and a card from Gina. Jack was hoeing into his pancakes with vigour.

"Woah, slow down there, mate," said Tony. "You're practically inhaling those things!"

Jack grinned at him.

"See the picture I made for Gab, Tony?" he said, pointing with his fork while his mouth was full of food.

"It's great, mate," said Tony. "I bet she loves it. Straight to the pool room for that one!" The picture was one of Gab and Jack riding bikes together, with *I luv yuo, Gab* painted across the top.

Gab put a cup of tea on the table in front of Tony with a plate of pancakes, bacon and maple syrup. She put the same down for herself as she had for Tony, and took a seat.

"Thanks, love. Looks fab. This a card from your mum?" He pointed at the card with sparkly kittens on the front. Gab nodded. "Mind if I take a look?" he asked. Gab shook her head. She didn't mind. Her mouth was full of pancakes and bacon too, just like her brother's.

Dear Gabrielle, my angel.

What would I do without you? You are my sunshine and my world. You are my everything.

Happy Birthday. I'm sorry I don't have the money to buy you anything. Things have been so hard over the last year. I'll make it up to you.

Love, Mum.

It made Tony sick, but he didn't want to hurt Gab by causing trouble on her birthday, so he put it down quietly and began his breakfast. Things weren't as hard as Gina made out, he thought to himself; or, if they were, she didn't realise how hard she made things for her daughter.

Secretly, Gab felt let down that her mum hadn't bothered to get her anything, though she'd promised to buy them take-away that night. All through the day she maintained a secret hope that Gina would spring something on her after all ... but by the end of the day, the possibility faded along with the evening light. Still, Gab was used to making the best of situations, and she was at least happy that Mum had given her a nice card, bought them dinner and had surprised her with a block of chocolate for dessert. Mum loved her; that was what mattered.

CHAPTER 13

Gab's new year was The Great Unknown. Why did it feel that way? She knew she'd be working roughly full-time at the local supermarket, and she knew she'd be looking after Jack and cooking dinner every night. The next milestone her peers were waiting for was university offers. They were being released mid-January, a week or so after Gab's eighteenth birthday. But uni offers weren't really on Gab's radar. It didn't matter whether she got into uni or not, because she couldn't go anyway—so she felt. She hadn't told Mr. C. that yet, or anyone else. But deep down she knew. She'd put in preferences because that was the expected thing to do, not because she'd been planning on going anywhere. It had felt like planning someone else's life, not hers; her path was already set. There wasn't really a choice. Jack needed her. So did her mum. Gab was aware of the Jack-factor in her decision; she was less aware of the sense of responsibility she felt for her mother. She didn't even know it was there. The weight of it had always sat upon her and she'd never known any different. For her, that's just how life was.

* * *

Another day, another shift at the supermarket. That was how Gab saw it. She pushed aside the thought of the university offer she had received that morning. It didn't make any difference—it was just another day.

Being a hot and blustery mid-January afternoon, the air-conditioned shop was a welcome change from both outdoors and the uninsulated granny-flat. Gab walked through the back door of the shop and into the tea-room with its kitchenette, putting her bag into a locker and donning her name badge and her checkout-girl persona. It was easy now, comfortable—not like when she'd first started. That had been terrifying and exhausting. She'd lie awake on Friday nights, terrified she'd miss her Saturday morning alarm and be late for her Saturday shift. And while working, she'd be so nervous she'd count back customers' change all wrong—even when the sum was easy. But now it was all second nature. Gab knew all the regulars. She wasn't fourteen years and nine months old anymore. She was an adult. Legally. This continued to surprise her.

Shoving a lolly into her mouth from the bowl on the tea-room table, she headed into the store.

"Hey Stacks!" called Jarrod from the deli, with the nickname he'd called her for years, ever since she'd begun stacking shelves.

"Hey Jarrod," she called back. Mac looked up from refilling the fruit display with bananas.

"You're on register two today, champ," he said with a jowly grin.

"Gotcha." Gab gave him a thumbs up and took her marks.

It was quiet today—far too hot for anyone to be doing much in the middle of the day—while smatterings of kids came through, buying all the ice-creams they could manage. Dirty hands smeared themselves over the ice-cream caddy, children counted out their pocket money for treats and most said "thank you" when they received their change. Gab felt proud of them when they did that.

4:51pm. Gab was clocking off at five o'clock. Busy wiping up after a dribbly pack of frozen peas on her conveyor belt, a quiet voice interrupted her thoughts.

"Hey, kiddo."

"Oh, hey Mr. C!" she smiled when she looked up to see him.

"You *can* call me James now, you know," he said. "School's over!"

"Ohhh nah, couldn't do that Mr. C!" she replied with a smirk.

"Course you can! You're an adult now and I'm not your teacher anymore."

"Maybe I'm an adult on the outside!" said Gab. He raised his eyebrows quizzically. "Besides," she teased, "you just called me *kiddo*!"

"I was being metaphorical."

"Sure, sure." Gab was bagging up his frozen corn cobs, a kilo of Grannie Smiths, a loaf of bread, two cartons of oat milk.

"Seriously though," he continued, "you've had more responsibility to shoulder than other kids your age." That one got her in the guts, so she focused on scanning his groceries fast as she could.

"Are you walking home, Mr. C?" she asked, before she could stop herself. He nodded and she continued: "I'm finishing my shift in... ," she checked her watch, "three minutes. Do you want to ... umm... I mean..." Why was this suddenly so difficult?

"Want to walk together? Great," he said easily. "Let's talk. I'll wait outside while you finish up." Gab nodded.

Mr. C (or *James*, as she couldn't bear to call him) took his bag of groceries and stood outside the front door. Elsy arrived to replace Gab at register two, and Gab went to get her bag. She joined Mr. C. out the front, her heart beating harder than she cared to admit. She didn't know why.

CHAPTER 14

The sun was setting and they walked quietly for a while, Gab pushing her bike alongside her. Mr. C. lived closer into the centre of town, while Gab lived another three kilometres out. She would walk him home. Gab was strangely glad for this simultaneously terrifying and happy moment that she didn't understand. She knew what she had to tell her teacher.

"So," said Mr. C. "I saw your results this morning. Straight into agriculture. Well done! I'm proud of you!" Gab's heart squeezed with strange warmth because no one had ever said that straight out to her before. But then the blood drained to her feet. It was a horrifying tension that she hid perfectly. She had to tell him.

"Thanks, Mr. C," she said tightly. "That's really nice." She felt numb.

"Agriculture, data science, psychology..." he continued, "Easily in. The world is your oyster." He paused. "Don't know where that one comes from. Weird saying, isn't it!"

"Shakespeare," Gab said. "It was first recorded in Shakespeare."

"Well, there you go!" said Mr. C.

He never seemed to mind when Gab taught *him* something, and Gab liked that. But then she remembered again what she had to tell him.

"Mr. C ... I ..." Gab sighed. She stopped and turned to face him. "Thanks for believing in me, Mr C. It means everything. But I'm not going." Then she quickly kept walking.

He paused for a moment, and then caught up with her. But she'd already made up her mind. It didn't even feel like there had been a decision to be made. It was a narrow trajectory; she was on it, and there was no swerving to the right or the left, no alternative path for diversion.

He was quiet. He nodded slowly. He didn't ask her why, but she answered anyway.

"I'm needed here."

Again, he nodded.

"I'll keep working. I've already increased my hours."

He was quiet. Gab's anger rose.

"What choice do I have?" she cried. "Mum needs me. Jack needs me. I can't desert them. I hate that I don't want to let you down. I hate that I want to live up to your hopes for me! Why do you even care?"

"Gab..." James sighed. This somehow made Gab angrier.

"You don't understand, Mr. C! Why are you doing this?" Gab started to cry and could have died from shame. Also, she knew he didn't deserve it and she had no idea where it was coming from ... quiet, sensible, measured Gab. The façade was gone.

"I'm sorry, Gabby," he whispered. "I'm really sorry. You need to do what's best, and it's your decision—no one else's."

"Anyway," Gab sniffed, wiping her eyes violently with her sleeve, "I'm not declining, just deferring. I can always go next year." She felt like she was lying, because she didn't see how it was possible.

"Melbourne's a fair way away, isn't it?" Mr. C. observed.

"I know," said Gab. "And I hate going away from home. But," she mused, "I don't really like being there either. So I guess I'm trapped." They were nearing Mr. Cheng's front gate.

"Have you thought about online study?" he asked. "I know we're a decent hike from any uni, but there are loads of distance ed. options. UNE for example. They offer an online Bachelor of Agriculture." He knew. He'd checked. He couldn't bear the thought of her wasting away in that granny flat for years to come.

Gab shook her head. "It's not the right time, Mr. C. My head's not in the right space."

"Oh well," he swallowed and smiled. "You'll make the best of it, Gab. You always do."

"Maybe," she replied, feeling sceptical.

"I know you will. Just keep reading. Keep learning. Don't let it crush you."

"I won't," Gab said. But she suddenly felt powerless. "You should probably just forget about me," she said, turning away and hopping on her bike. She rode a couple of metres, not looking back, leaving Mr. Cheng at his front gate. Then she felt bad and turned to look at him. He was standing where she'd left him. Gab rolled her eyes, because she knew she couldn't just keep going with things like this. Swallowing her absurd embarrassment, she rolled back.

"I'm sorry. I just ..."

"It's okay, Gab," he assured her. "You don't have to explain." He paused and changed tack entirely. "So, what's on the menu for dinner tonight?"

Just like that, the whole outburst may as well not have happened; it was swallowed up in the past. It was good that way; Gab wouldn't have known what else to say.

"Spag Bol, I think." Mundane discussion was a relief.

"Sounds great," he said. "Thanks for the walk, Gab." He smiled, as if her embarrassing explosion had never happened; as if her choice to defer her studies and spend her nineteenth year working in the supermarket hadn't hit him like a punch in the guts too.

CHAPTER 15

Gab lay on her bed that night with hot tears spilling down her face. There was a rending pain somewhere inside her—she didn't know exactly where. It was all because of that stupid evening conversation with Mr. C.

Gab's journal lay in front of her. She felt compelled to write about what had happened; she needed detangling. And she felt so guilty.

At the bottom of her journal entry, in big letters, she wrote:

I AM NOT REJECTING THE OFFER. I AM JUST DEFERRING. I'LL GO NEXT YEAR.

"I'm lying. It'll never happen," she said to herself aloud, slapping her journal shut. But Gina was in the room next door and heard.

"What was that, dear?" her mum squawked through the wall. Gab rolled her eyes.

"Nothing, Mum! Don't WORRY!"

She flicked open her journal again and wrote words that didn't even feel like hers. *Would that woman just leave me alone and stop inflicting her anxieties on me!! It's bloody stifling!*

But then she felt guilty about that too.

"You're meant to make me feel better," she said to her journal. Then she threw it across the room and hid under the blankets, trying not to think anymore.

"What was that, Gabrielle?" came the inevitable inquiry.

* * *

It wasn't unusual for kids at Gab's school to take a gap year between high school and uni. Still, those who knew Gab—her teachers, her work colleagues, her peers—were somewhat surprised by her choice to do so. But this was the decision that didn't feel like a decision. It may have looked like a choice to those on the outside, but to Gab, there was no question. Jack had turned seven and was starting Grade 2. Gina was as needy as ever, not that Gab would have described it that way. Gab felt needed and had a role to play. For some reason—one not even conscious to her, but perhaps having something to do with Mr. Cheng being an alumnus there—she had her heart set on a prestigious university in Melbourne. She didn't want to think about other options; there were too many and it was overwhelming. This at least had narrowed things down. And the university she wanted to attend didn't offer a Bachelor of Agriculture online or by distance. Being at home, she had more important things to think about anyhow. She had to look after Jack, and work. How else could they afford to send him to swimming lessons and to other kids' birthday parties? Gab was aspirational and loved to challenge herself, but her own education could take a backseat. Her family gave her purpose. And work (and the money that came with it) increased her sense of independence. It didn't bother her to stay in town working. What bothered her was when people around her talked to her about it and acted surprised that she wasn't going to uni, especially after her Year 12 results. It annoyed her intensely; how could they understand the responsibilities that were hers? Who were they to judge?

She knew her high school friends had whispered about her mother sometimes, with words like 'needy' and 'demanding'; she had felt mortified and guilty of some unnamed crime when in Year

12 psychology class, they had discussed 'co-dependence'. Then, that word was added to the arsenal of judgment used by the other kids as they tried to diagnose Gab's situation for her, both secretly and not-so-secretly. What could Gab do about it? Why were her family relationships labelled as unhealthy when she didn't know any different? And what would it mean for her future? Why did she feel like there was something wrong with her when she was just being herself? It was so unfair.

These thoughts and fears had been woven into her final year of schooling, sometimes surfacing visibly, but often running under the surface. Now, Gab's work at the supermarket was a relief, a continuity. A relief all the more because she shrunk at the thought of spending countless days at home with her mother. But Mac had said she could work thirty or more hours a week, mostly during school hours and on every second weekend when Jack was staying with his dad in the next town along. And she was planning to help Tony on the farm with a whole lot of tree planting, in the hope of regenerating some of the areas decimated by decades upon decades of cattle farming. That was a plan, wasn't it?

CHAPTER 16

April

Gab was dreaming about building a brilliant treehouse. Suddenly, she woke to a half-scream. She was instantly on alert, ears pricked in the dark night. What was it? Maybe just a moody koala? They did have an awful sound. She hadn't caught enough of the sound with her conscious mind to really trust her sense of judgement. She didn't want to over-react ... but neither did she want to under-react if something was seriously wrong.

Then, Gab heard a strange bang-bang-bang from Gina's room. Her heart began pounding against her tight chest. She didn't want to know what was happening, but how could she pretend not to have heard?

"Mum?" she called out timidly. "Mum? Are you okay?" No answer. What if someone had broken in? It was just her and Jack and Gina in the house; Tony was up the hill, too far away to be of instant help. She could phone him ... but that would mean making noise. Perhaps she should tiptoe quietly to Gina's room first and find out what was going on without being seen.

There wasn't far to go. Gab tiptoed noiselessly, holding her breath, until she reached her mother's door. It was slightly ajar. Gab realised her plan wasn't really a good one; there was no way she could open the door further without being seen. She should have grabbed a weapon first! But she was too far gone now. So she pushed the door ever so gently, hoping to goodness things were alright.

It was only Gina in the room after all. She stood at her window in the moonlight, her silhouette framed in its reflected rays, her hair dishevelled, her floral silk kimono awry.

"Are you alright, Mum?"

"Alright? Why would I be alright?" her mother snarled. Then she moaned an awful moan. "Hopeless! It's all hopeless! I may as well be dead!"

Gab's stomach dropped. Her mum wasn't a go-getter, but she had never been this direct before.

"What's hopeless, Mum?" asked Gab, coming in and sitting on the bed to steady herself. She still couldn't make sense of the situation. "Don't say that."

Gina was holding her head in her hands.

"I can't do it Gab! I can't! It's not safe here." She looked suddenly at her daughter, her face tear-streaked and desperate. "I woke up and sensed a strong presence of evil in here, Gab," she whispered hoarsely. "Evil is present, and I can feel its influence on me."

"What do you *mean*, Mum?" cried Gab in fright. "Did you hear something? Is there someone around the house?"

"Not some*one*, Gabrielle," whispered her mother. "Some*thing*".

Gab felt like her body was turning inside-out. Her heart had squeezed down so tightly there was none of it left; her mother was a conduit of terror. Was Gina thinking straight? Should Gab trust her? Were they in danger? Gab couldn't make sense of any of it; this was beyond Gina's usual fetishes and eccentricities.

"What should I do, Mum?" choked Gab, as the hysteria caught hold of her.

"Wake Jack," said Gina. "We've got to get out."

So Gab, under the influence of her mother's persuasive illusions, woke her brother.

"Jack, wake up!" she whispered urgently.

Jack didn't stir, and Gab's terror compounded.

"Jack? Jack?!"

"*Whaaaat?*" he groaned. "Is it time to get up yet?"

"No ... I mean, yes. Come on Jack, get up!"

"Why?"

"Mum says we're in danger!" Suddenly Jack was up.

"Why, Gab?" he asked. "Where?" Then he started to cry. "I'm scared!"

Gab helped him put on a top and a pair of shorts.

"It's okay, Jack," said Gab, holding her brother close and making a Herculean effort to steel herself against her terror so that she could lie for her brother's sake. She guided him into Gina's room. Gina was lying on the bed now. *Why is she lying on the bed?* wondered Gab. *Didn't they have to leave?*

"Mum?" whispered Gab. "Jack's here. What do we do now?"

"What do you mean?" her mum barked.

"You said we were in danger."

"Oh, that!" Gina waved her hand as though she were swatting a fly. Gab frowned. Nothing about this night was making sense.

"Mum? Jack's here. We're ready. What should we do?"

"Just go back to bed," said Gina. Gab couldn't read the tone of her voice. Never in Gab's life had her mind had to work so hard at piecing together a situation.

"But Mum ..."

"GO. BACK. TO. BED!" Gina yelled.

Gab had no choice. Things had flipped ... again. But there was no way she was going back into her room alone. She wasn't leaving Jack alone either. Gab led him back to his bed and snuggled in next to him, fitting in the small space between his nimble body and the wall. She held him close.

"What happened?" asked Jack.

"Oh, must have been a false alarm, mate," said Gab, steadying her voice. "Mum must've got a fright but then realised it was nothing. Maybe she just had a bad dream."

"Oh, phew," said Jack. "That was scary." Gab agreed with the entirety of her being, but didn't show it.

"It's okay Jack, go back to sleep."

"Gab? I'm still a bit scared. Can you tell me a story?" How the hell was Gab meant to manage this? There was nothing there, her mind was blank. So she opened her mouth and began with some random words.

"Once upon a time, there was a wombat who lived down at the creek bed ... "

Beginning was the hardest part; after she had begun, the story began to tell itself, carrying her along with it as if it were being told to her as much she was telling it. Thankfully, it didn't take Jack long to fall back to sleep. He was good like that. But Gab didn't doze off for hours, and then, the sleep only came in disrupted fits, ending suddenly with the echoes of a disrupted scream. What had happened? She didn't know.

CHAPTER 17

It happened again, two weeks later. A scream woke her in the night. Gab moved into Jack's room permanently after that, as much as for herself as for him, though she was hardly aware of any reasoning behind the decision. It was automatic, triggered by a stimulus that led to a prewired response, without conscious cognition entering the equation. Just like deferring uni. Gab shivered when she thought of Jack left at home with her mum, enduring a night like the one that had just passed. Imagine if he'd been the one who had woken up; who had found Gina in her room with her pills; who had again heard her sense of the great evil present in their home. Gab wondered if it was true about the evil. Deferring uni—yes, she had done the right thing, definitely.

* * *

Gina sat cross-legged on her worn cushions, a shrine set up on the coffee table before her. A picture of Jesus sat next to a small, grey Buddha statue (purchased from the local two-dollar shop), while rosary beads and crystals were laid out around the figures. Incense sticks burned in a small pot of sand. Fruit and a few flowers had been laid on the shrine as a gift to the gods and Gina was writing on little, torn bits of paper. Some small scribblings were prayers; she laid them out with the flowers and fruits. On other pieces of paper, Gina wrote words which represented the evil spirits she was casting out of her and her children's lives (or trying to). Those pieces she would scrunch up and place in the pot of sand, setting them smouldering with the incense sticks. That was meant to banish the visceral dread and despair, projected as evil pressing in on the house, that she felt when darkness began to fall ...

Gina had always been difficult, but things were intensifying. Her primary shortcoming was a complete lack of engagement with her children's needs. It was as if her kids were just too much, so she shut herself off, in her own world of thought, prayer and self-justification. Her narrative on the world both shaped and reflected her unwillingness to connect with her kids or to take on challenges—to persist when the going got tough. And that was because for her, the going was always tough and any additional challenge threatened, she thought, to break her rather than to make her stronger. And besides, she just didn't *want* to engage. Her religious sensibilities, her engagement in her perceived 'spiritual world', her pronouncements on the state of the universe—all these things were, to her, more important than the flesh and blood, the pulsating hearts and growing minds around her. It was the concrete reality of life that was to her ethereal, and her eclectic world of spirits, forces, gods and ideologies was most real. But the more she absorbed herself in it, the more she lost her grip on reality—or perhaps it was the other way around, or perhaps it was both. She was flesh and blood too, as much as she tried—for whatever reasons—to avoid this fact.

Her upbringing had not been easy, admittedly. She'd been adopted and, while she had moved into a loving family, she'd still felt inferior to her siblings—not because of anything her parents had done, but because she felt her difference. Her adoptive father had died when she was twelve; her mother Betty, a kindly church lady and diligent housewife, had been her one support as she grew up. After Gina had had Gab, Betty visited the granny flat every day. It was Betty who had raised Gab for her first three years. She had been loving, responsive, nurturing—all the things the small Gab needed. But then Betty's health had taken a sharp turn, and it was a steep decline. She died when Gab was five, and then Gab and Gina were alone, because Gina, with her difficult personality, had become estranged from her two adoptive siblings.

Gina had always been searching for something more to life, for its meaning, for explanations for the things that happened, as though explanations would make life more manageable. But she didn't tend to look for explanations in the most helpful places. She was suspicious and superstitious, and made wild connections between unrelated occurrences and minor contingencies. She shaped her own world of cause-and-effect, disconnected from those around her. And she was always the victim. This reflected and perpetuated her sense of powerlessness.

Tony often wondered in frustration why Gina couldn't just 'get things together'. How hard was it to get out of that room, to go along to a parent-teacher interview at school, or to a school awards night? But for Gina, it was impossible; she'd built a wall in her mind that entirely devalued those things, and entirely elevated her internal musings in that sunroom kingdom. Besides, the world out there was a big, bad place to her, and she felt much more able to change it by chanting incantations and offering prayers in her sunroom than by stepping out into it. Where does health start and illness begin? Where do difficult circumstances cease to be an excuse, and at what point is someone to be held responsible for their actions and decisions? Was it mental illness or choice? How much agency did Gina have in this scenario?

Labels became barriers to hide behind; it was easier to set up camp under their banner than to press forward. And Gina really did feel powerless, she felt like a victim—there was no dishonesty in that. She didn't have any sense that help was out there for her, or a willingness to reach out for it. It didn't seem an option because she didn't want to change. It was more comfortable to keep things how they were. Yes, she attended doctor's appointments frequently; so frequently. But strangely, this fed into her spiral. For her children, Gina's behaviour was problematic and painful. Gab felt responsible to fix it all and she couldn't. Her mother had become her burden, her care, long ago—before she had the age and maturity to realise that it wasn't her fault.

CHAPTER 18

June

"Gabrielle?"

"Yes, Mum?" said Gab, popping her head into the sunroom, having just put some veggies on to roast.

"I'm *really* sorry, Gabby, but ... can I pleeeease borrow $50? Just for a bit—I'll pay it back on pension day, I promise."

Gab's desire to help her mum wrestled with frustration. This was the third time in a fortnight.

"Mum, you haven't paid me back that other $80 yet," said Gab.

"*Gaaab*," whined Gina. "I'm your *mother*! I just," Gina bit her lip in self-generated distress, "it's really hard, okay? I've never had much money ... "

"I know, Mum," sighed Gab. "I'm sorry. It's just that I'm saving up as much as I can and ... "

"I'll give it all back to you on pension day, Gab—I *promise*. I promise!"

"Okay Mum, I'll transfer the money to your account now." That was the quickest way to do it.

In truth, Gina didn't need it, no matter how much she thought she did. Or at least, she needed it for her own sense of fulfilment, but this was not in any accord with Gab's goals and needs. Gina was using the money for online tarot readings and sessions with a spiritual healing coach. She had become convinced that she could find answers for her unquenchable existential discomfort, for her mental ill-health, if she could somehow get to the source of it all. The tarot readings were addictive, and now her monthly instalment for the coaching was due.

When the roast had cooked, Gab brought Gina her meal in the sunroom.

"Thanks honey," said Gina with a big sigh.

"Are you alright, Mum?" asked Gab, worried, but also *not* wanting to know the answer.

"Oh, my body is just not interested in food at the moment." Gina sighed yet again. "Everything I eat ... bloating and more bloating. Acid reflux too." She shook her head as Gab barely hid a grimace. "I'm sure it's a sign of spiritual distress," concluded Gina.

"Why?" asked Gab, frowning.

"The body expresses the truth of the spirit," said Gina knowingly. "Fix the spirit, and you fix the body."

Gab wondered if it was true.

"So, you don't want your dinner, Mum? Go on, you'll feel better if you have some. Just a little bit?"

"Leave it here, Gab," said Gina, as though she were making a painful concession. "I'll try."

So Gab did. Gina's lack of interest in food worried her. Gab would collect Gina's dinner plate from the sunroom each evening, and there was often two-thirds of every meal still on the plate. Gab wondered what it meant, and whether her mother was right about disruptions in a person's spirit outworking themselves in that person's body. She wondered what she could do to help her mother.

Gina had been a regular at the local GP for years, visiting at least once a fortnight with one complaint or another. That was why Gab hated going to the doctor's—she never went for herself, but she had childhood memories of lying on the thick, shaggy carpet in the doctor's waiting room, watching cooking show reruns on the TV there—and of hunching in the corner of the doctor's room, pretending to play with the toys, while her mum told the doctor all the things that were wrong with her, what her latest symptoms were, why it was more serious than the doctor was willing to credit. Gab had stopped going on those visits as soon as Gina let her stay home by herself, when she was eight years old.

But now Gina was resisting going to the doctor, which Gab thought was strange. At least with her frequent visits to the GP, Gina was being checked on regularly. But she hadn't been for months. Gab asked her mother about it the next morning.

"You haven't been to the doctor in ages, Mum. Why don't you go for a checkup?"

Gina just sighed and slumped back in her chair, her eyes closed.

"Dr. Waterfall is on leave. I'm not interested in talking to anyone else," she said in a monotone voice.

"How long is he gone for?" asked Gab.

"Months. He's taking long service leave," said Gina, eyes still closed.

"But couldn't you go see the replacement doctor?"

"No!" Gina's eyes flicked open.

"Why not?" Gab pressed.

"Gabrielle!" Now Gina leaned forward in her chair, finally animated—which Gab preferred to the still, quiet, numb figure of a moment before. "I do *not* need a doctor. Not a physical doctor. Traditional medicine does not have all the answers!". Which was a strange thing for Gina to say, Gab thought, because she relied on that concoction of 'traditional medicine' to get her through each day. Suddenly Gina screamed, "GO GABBY!! JUST GO!!" in a flurry of desperation, and Gab quickly backed out and shut the door. She wouldn't say anything more about it.

CHAPTER 19

August

Gab was on high alert now and it never stopped. She still slept in Jack's room, as Gina's search for spiritual answers to her existential hunger took her down ever more convoluted routes. She wanted answers, she wanted 'healing' (as she called it), she wanted to find her true self. She was absolutely convinced that revelation or enlightenment or zen or nirvana—whatever she chose to call it—was right around the corner. She lived her life in anticipation of looking around that next corner and finding the answer ... only then to discover another corner that perhaps offered a better answer.

It was not uncommon for Gab to wake to noises in the night now, as Gina tossed and turned and fussed and spoke her strange prayers aloud. Jack had picked up on things too; it was impossible for him not to, and as much as Gab tried to shield him from it all, Jack also sensed her own anxiety, her edginess. Gab was worried about what he would tell Brian—not that she wanted to keep it all a secret, but she was afraid of the consequences. Mostly, she felt an impermeable impetus to protect her mother, to protect her mother's reputation despite everything, and to protect the current structure of their home. What else did they have? Besides, she was the one dealing with it all; she could handle it and she would protect Jack. But Brian did hear strange stories from Jack about Gina's erratic behaviour, and about Gab sleeping in his room and getting up at odd hours of the night.

It was a dark August night—winter, and cold. Gab had taken to waking with a jerk even when there was no noise, but this time, she was sure she'd heard one. Did she need to check? It was so warm in bed and so cold out there.

She thought she heard Gina shuffling down the passageway and turning on the kitchen light. Then she heard her shuffling back towards her room again; the door closed and the gentle clink of the hook in the eyelet signified the door having been locked. Gab was up in a flash, tiptoeing to her mother's bedroom door. She knocked gently.

"Mum?"

No answer.

"Mum?" Gab's heart was racing. "You okay?" Gina had become unpredictable; Gab had no idea what she might be planning to do. Gab was pretty sure she wouldn't ...

After thirty seconds of silence, Gab turned around and tiptoed to the kitchen. Maybe she'd be able to see what Gina had taken from there. She'd check that the knives were in place; that was the first thing. She flicked on the kitchen light.

Yes, knives in the knife block all present and accounted for. Just to be safe, she'd hide them in her bedroom. It would be an inconvenience when cooking dinner, but it would take a significant weight off her mind. She'd been toying with the idea of quietly confiscating the knives for ages, but it made the danger seem so real that she'd avoided it. Now it was time.

But first things first; why had Gina been in here? Maybe she'd just been getting a drink of water? A hot water bottle? Maybe ... Gab scanned the room and her eyes rested on the top of the refrigerator. Gina's medicine tub was gone. It was always usually there, waiting for Gina as soon as she got up in the morning to take her concoction of medications designed to keep her functional, if not well. But it wasn't there, and Gab felt heavy darkness slice right through her. *Not again*. She ran back to her mother's room.

"Mum? Mum, answer me!" she whispered urgently.

"Go away, Gabrielle."

"No, Mum. I know you've got your pills in there. Why have you got them?"

"None of your business."

"Have you got a headache? Are you taking Panadol?"

Gina pulled open the door a crack. She had locked it by slipping the little hook into its eyelet. Gab could see a sliver of her mother's face, her bulging eye, her glistening skin.

"No, Gab," she said, as if she was talking to someone whom she thought was very unintelligent. "I haven't got a headache. I've locked myself in my room *with my pills*. What do you *think* I'm going to do?!" Then Gina shut the door.

Gab began to retch, then ran to the kitchen to grab a butterknife, trying to swallow what Gina had just said. She was going to get into her mother's room and get those pills, and nothing was going stop her! Butterknife in hand, she was back at her mother's door in the blink of an eye. She tried to open it a slit again, but Gina was leaning against it.

"Mum! Mum!" Gab whispered urgently. She did *not* want Jack to wake up and witness any of this, but apart from her voice, how else was she going to convince her mother to let her in right now?

No answer.

"MUM! Answer me!!" cried Gab, still trying to restrain herself to a whisper. But her mother would neither answer nor move.

CHAPTER 20

Gab suddenly had an idea. She ran to the front door, not even bothering to put gumboots on, pulled it open and raced round to the side of the house where Gina's bedroom window faced out. As the granny flat was on a slope, the window was too high for Gab to climb in through it without a ladder. But she scooped up a handful of gravel and let a spray of it fly at the window.

"What the?" The sound of the gravel hitting the window distracted Gina. Gab let fly another handful and then pressed herself against the wall. She could run up to Tony's ... but she had to get those pills first. She watched Gina's window with her heart racing and saw Gina approaching it to look out and find the source of the noise.

"Gab! Gabby! Are you out there?" called Gina. "Is that you?" Suddenly she sounded frightened. And this was Gab's chance. Quick as lightning, she raced back around and into the house, through the front door, back up the passageway to Gina's bedroom door. She picked up the butterknife from the floorboards where she had left it, pushed the door open as far as it would go while it was locked and slipped the knife through the crack, flicking the hook out of the eyelet in a flash.

She was in!

"Mum!"

"Gab! Was that you outside? Was it?" Gina shrieked.

"Mum … give me those pills." Gab put out her hand and Gina frowned, holding the box of pills tight against her. She was too caught up in her own torrential emotion to notice Gab's hand shaking violently.

"No," Gina said. "They're mine."

"I know they're yours Mum. I'm not taking them permanently. Just for now. You don't need them at the moment, do you?"

"How do you know what I need?" Gina snapped.

"Well, I don't Mum, but if you tell me what you need, I can help you!"

Gina shook her head stubbornly, like an obstinate child.

"Mum, seriously," pleaded Gab. "For Jack's sake! Holding onto them isn't going to solve anything. Just … please!" said Gab. Then she started to cry.

Suddenly Gina's bottom lip started to tremble. It wasn't so much that she was moved by the feelings she had evoked in her daughter, as that she couldn't bear to see someone else as centre of attention; it was *her* feelings that were real and important … *hers!*

"Gaaaab!" she moaned, "I don't know why you're making such a big deal of this! Why do you always give me such a hard time?" Then Gina slumped onto the bed, still grasping her pills but with less re-solve. Gab was beside herself, beginning to dissociate, beginning to retreat to that position right up in the top of her skull where it was dreamland, and she didn't live in her body anymore. Mechanically, she saw her chance and grabbed the tub of pills from her mother's arms. Her young, wiry arms, whose strength was built in digging on the farm, carrying her brother, and through years of climbing trees, were more than a match for her mother's—as were her speedy reflexes. The relief crashed over her.

"Right, Mum," she said. "I'm … I'm looking after these from now on, and I'll give you your medicine each morning." She would buy a locker for the pills.

Gina sat up again and crossed her arms moodily. "No fair!" she said to Gab huffily. "Why do you have to take things so seriously? I was just joking around!"

Gab's jaw dropped.

That was it. It was more than Gab could take. Those pills were going in the bin. She didn't care. She'd had a gut full. She stormed outside, Gina tottering after her, whining and pleading and trying to catch her daughter's arm and grab back her pills. But Gab was lithe and quick; much too fast for Gina, and in no time, she'd reached the big skip that sat in the paddock beside the driveway and had thrown the entire box in. There was no way Gina could get them back, amongst the debris of weeks-old trash. They were gone.

Then Gab ran back to the house, and left Gina wailing outdoors in the moonlight. She shut the door to Jack's room, shoved a chair under the handle so that Gina couldn't get in, and lay on the floor an empty shell.

CHAPTER 21

September

"What the hell do you mean, *Jack's gone*??"

Gab had arrived home from work that evening to find Jack's room empty, his clothes and toys gone. Gina sat passively at the kitchen table. Vague. Empty.

"Brian wants full custody," Gina shrugged. "He picked up Jack while you were at work. He's going to keep him 'til court."

"And you didn't think it was relevant to tell me about this earlier?!" Gab was livid. "Had you and Brian talked about this??"

Years of suppressed fury washed over her in waves.

"*I* am the one who looks after him! I cook his food, I wash his clothes, I take him to school," she cried. "And suddenly you tell me that Brian wants full custody?!!" She was pacing like mad; she didn't know which way to turn.

"I didn't know it would actually happen," whined Gina. "Brian's all talk. He's been saying this for years. I didn't think he'd actually *do* anything about it."

"Yeah?!" Gab cried, suddenly realising something new despite her disorientation. "Well, I'm GLAD Brian's taken Jack. I'm GLAD!"

Gina made her 'shock' face with all the authenticity of a mime.

"You mean you don't *want* to look after your baby brother anymore?" Gina asked. "Gabrielle, I'm surprised!"

"NO Mum, NO! That's not it. How dare you!" Gab yelled. "Brian *deserves* Jack. Jack deserves a good home. At least Brian *acts* like a parent!" Gab stormed towards the front door.

"What is *that* supposed to mean?" yelled her mother in retort.

"You even have to *ask*?!! I cannot BELIEVE you are so *oblivious*!" Gab was blind with rage and disbelief.

"I have *health* issues!" her mother's voice was finally rising too, and she stood up from the table. Gab was glad. It was better than that infernal equilibrium that was less like calm and more like infinite nothingness.

"You have care-factor issues!" Gab jabbed, turning before she walked out the door. "You don't CARE—about Jack *or me*!"

Gina huffed and puffed; she glared at Gab. She did not respond. And then, she closed her eyes, held her hands together in prayer and glided towards the sunroom. Down, down, down; she was sinking back into her ocean of passivity. This was the last straw.

"Stuff you, Mum!" cried Gab, slamming the door as knives of guilt stabbed through her on a thousand different angles.

CHAPTER 22

Jack didn't need her anymore. Gab knew it. Not in the same way, anyhow. Brian would win custody; Gab decided she would even help him do it. Jack was safe at Brian's, and he was happy there. He deserved that. And she hoped it would hurt her mum. But she was filled with a flooding resentment at the thought that Gina would simply attribute it all to the gods, to fate or to whatever suited her latest penchant for avoiding reality. Gina refused to realise her own agency.

There was no point hanging around. Gab was free. She had been pushed so far that she just couldn't care anymore. Gab was sick of it, literally sick. So, after walking the paddocks for hours and then lying in Tony's hammock under his veranda until dark, Gab walked silently back to her room. She went to her shelf and pulled out last year's University handbook. As it was September, her re-enrolment letter should be arriving in the next couple of months. She could take up her place after the year-long deferral.

A Bachelor of Agriculture. Now she allowed herself to really imagine it, to place herself there. She read through the first-year units: *Foundations of Agricultural Science, Agriculture in Australia, Biology, Plant production systems, Animal production systems* ... She knew she'd love it; she was hungry for it. Her mind was a new place.

She didn't tell Gina what she was planning. They didn't talk. Gab began spending her evenings after work in Tony's hammock or in his lounge-room, planning and researching.

She'd be moving to Melbourne. She needed somewhere to live. But her eyeballs nearly fell out of her head when she saw the prices of university onsite accommodation. Then she checked places further away from the university. Slightly more affordable—but only because Gab had spent a whole year working and saving.

"Well, Mr. C," she said aloud to herself, as she lay in the hammock one evening, "good thing I worked this year after all! Imagine living in the city with no savings!"

Gab was nervous about finding her way into and around the city. She could do so much for herself already, but she felt like a country mouse when it came to moving out. She'd only been into Melbourne a handful of times on school excursions. Her mum certainly never took her on outings or taught her to navigate terrain beyond their own town. But Gab was wholly determined to do it.

By the end of the week, she had a long list of accommodation options. On Saturday morning, she sat down and tried to make a shortlist. By lunchtime, she needed a break and took a ride down to the shops for a blue sports drink and a pie. Riding back, her mind worked as hard in filtering the mental overload as her legs did in pumping the pedals. Against the grain of the hoarding nature instilled in her by a life of poverty, Gab decided (by the time she got home) that what she would look for a middle-of-the-road sharehouse. A couple of hundred dollars a week would be manageable. That eliminated the top-notch accommodation, which was never really an option anyway, and the dead-cheap single rooms that looked about as big as a cereal box. Those could wait for next year, if and when her money ran out. If she could find a part-time job in the city, that would help too. Her work experience put her in good stead.

Satisfied with her decision, she worked through her short-list and began the online applications. That made it frighteningly real. Fingers crossed something would work out. Send. Send. Send. And more sending. Nine applications sent by dinnertime. It would be cheese on toast tonight. She had more important things to be doing than cooking. Did it matter that the re-enrolment letter hadn't come yet? She felt nervous about it, but surely it would come?

September

It came. This was the missing piece in the puzzle—the letter telling Gab that it was now time to enrol for next year, if she wanted to take up the offer of a place in the Bachelor of Agriculture course. When it came, Gab held the letter in her hands and kissed it—her ticket to freedom. She ran up the hill to Tony's and found him under the veranda, attaching a new handle to one of his shovels.

"Tony!" she cried, out of breath, "I'm going to uni!"

"What's that, love?" he called as he looked up, swatting flies away from his sweaty face.

"Uni!" Gab cried, "I'm going to start my Agriculture degree next year! Look!" And she showed him the letter that proved her place had indeed been held.

"Oh, good on you, love! It came!" he said. "I knew it would. It's about time something good happened for you." Tony had been relieved when Brian came to take Jack, but he'd feared for Gab alone with Gina. He didn't want to judge, and he didn't know the details of the dramas that were unfolding, but he was sure Brian was a damn site more qualified to care for his son than Gina was. And Gab was caught in the middle.

"I guess you can relax a bit now that Jack's with Brian?" Tony half-enquired, as he resumed sanding the new handle.

"Yeah," agreed Gab. "He's way happier there. Will you ... will you keep an eye on Mum for me when I'm gone?" That sad, lost, beholden part of her that still existed felt obliged to ask.

"You know I will, Gab," said Tony. "Though what I really wish is that she'd look after *herself*." He saw Gab's face fall. "Still," he said, regretting his loose tongue, "I'm sure she'll be fine without you, love. You've gotta make your own way forward, don't you?"

"You should see the subjects I get to do next year, Tony! They're awesome! And I'll fill you in on everything I learn."

"Can't wait to hear about it, love. Is there anything you need? When are you leaving?"

"Well, I found a stack of shared apartments to apply for," explained Gab. "So, I just have to wait and see what happens with that. I don't *think* I need anything ... but I'll let you know."

"How 'bout I drive you down to town when you move in? Saves you taking all your stuff on the bus."

"Oh, yeah! That'd be great. Thanks Tony."

"Any time, love."

Gab ran off again with more spring in her step than she'd had in a long, long time. She was going to phone Mr. C. and tell him too. He'd be delighted.

CHAPTER 24

Gina and Gab still weren't talking. Since the blow up when Gab had said she was leaving, Gina had refused to even acknowledge her. Gab actually found it a relief. She didn't have to put up with Gina's wheedling, her put-downs, her whining. When one of Gab's applications for a shared apartment was accepted, it all became so real. The countdown was on. While Gab was nervous as anything, she was also so ready that nothing could stop her. She threw herself into her final months of work at the supermarket, picking up extra shifts to bump up her savings and working as much as she could over the Christmas and New Year period.

Jack cried when Gab told him that she was leaving. She assured him she would call him often, and Brian promised he'd drive Jack down to visit Gab in Melbourne. Jack was mollified by this, and adapted to the idea quickly, after the initial shock.

The evening in mid-February before she left, she rode around to Mr. C's place to say goodbye. She'd seen him regularly throughout the year, usually at the checkout at work. Once, he'd invited her to come and talk to his current Year 12 students, giving them top maths study tips and exam preparation ideas. And a few weeks ago, Mr. C. and his wife Melinda had invited Gab around for dinner. Gab was simultaneously terrified and chuffed.

It was bizarre and intriguing seeing Mr. C. at home with his family. Gab had seen them all together before around town and at school events like the fundraising fair. But this was different. It was home.

James and Melinda Cheng had two young children, Libby and Tyler, aged five and three. Watching Mr. C. interact with his children thoughtfully, lovingly, attentively, wakened something inside Gab that she didn't know was there. Riding home, she felt sadder than ever in her life before. She had seen something entirely new, and it brought on a deep existential pain that began somewhere just under her heart and flowed into every limb and extremity. There was a jealous grief mingled with pain; jealousy, that those children had got Mr. C. as their father, and that she hadn't. She would have given anything to be them and not her. She tried quickly to bat that illogical, embarrassing feeling away. But it very quickly seemed to have intertwined itself with every fibre and cell of her body, as a deep, heavy longing. She couldn't *not* feel it, unless she blocked it out and went into numb-mode. Yet something about this feeling repelled the numbness, the numbness that had always been Gab's retreat. She was waking up. And the intense pain also showed her that she was alive, that she was *there* somewhere after all, hidden underneath all the mess and tangle of getting through daily life with its perpetual dramas. She *cared*.

On the morning of her move to Melbourne, Gab knocked on the Cheng's front door with a fluttering heart. Mr. C. was so pleased to see her take up the opportunity. He didn't let on how much. He didn't want to crowd Gab or intrude. Nevertheless, when he opened the door, he heartily wished her every good thing, reminding her that if she ever wanted to check in, he was only a phone call away. He'd watched her grow from a timid, acquiescent eleven-year-old, to a deeply aspirational, sensitive adult. He told her this, and he told her he was proud of her. Gab left feeling like she had been filled to overflowing with something light and warm and energising

—as though she had been filled with something like life. For a few moments, it banished all second-guessing and fear.

Gab rode home and finished loading up the car with Tony. It didn't take long. When she bade goodbye to Gina, her mother hardly blinked. Gab might as well have been off to work. But that was okay, Gab thought. She preferred that to a grovelling, wailing mess of a mother. After a phone call with Jack and Brian, Gab left with the strangest bag of mixed feelings swirling within her.

CHAPTER 25

Mid-February

Gab sat in her new room for the first time, after Tony had helped her move in with her small collection of things. She studied her timetable and a map. Gab feared becoming lost, being late, looking imbecilic. It was a big place this university, let alone the whole city, compared with the small town she'd grown up in—the primary school with a hundred kids, and the secondary school with about the same.

There was a quiet knock on Gab's door. She went and unlocked it, opening it to find one of her new housemates, Freya. Freya's big dark eyes looked enquiringly at Gab's sheepish grey ones.

"Hi Gab," she said, with an awkward little wave.

"Hi," said Gab shyly. "Do you want to come in?"

Freya nodded and took a few steps into her room.

"Wow, this is coming along nicely!" she said, referring to Gab's room.

"Thanks," said Gab, perking up a little. "I think it's all set up."

"Looks great," smiled Freya. "Love your plants!"

"Oh, yeah, thanks," said Gab. "I'm studying agriculture, so ..." she shrugged.

"Great! I'm in my second year of a Bachelor of Design. Are you just starting?"

Gab nodded. "I deferred last year. I think we're at the same uni?"

"Cool," said Freya, smiling. "Hey … how are your cooking skills?"

Gab shrugged again. "Alright, I guess," she answered, underselling herself. "I always cook at home."

"Good," said Freya. "Because we've got a weekly cooking roster. Everyone takes a turn. We're a bit nerdy and organised here!"

"Sure," said Gab. "I'll cook."

"Thanks!" said Freya, "Do you have a preference for any night in particular?"

"No," said Gab, "any night is fine with me."

"I'll slot you in on Tuesdays then," said Freya. "That's when Emily, our last housemate, used to cook. Tonight's fend-for-yourself-night—that's what we do on the weekends—but I'm making a big curry. You're welcome to have some if you like?"

"Okay, yes please," Gab was quietly relieved. She hadn't even thought about food yet.

"Any food allergies? No? Easy. Oh, we've also got chores divvied up between us too. Can you take on Emily's? She used to give the kitchen a once-over on the weekends, and vacuum the lounge once a week."

"Of course, sure," said Gab. Then Freya explained who else did what and when, and the consequences if jobs weren't done.

"Steph forgot to take out the rubbish a fortnight ago," explained Freya. "So she had to wear her undies on the outside when she took the rubbish out last week. And my job is cleaning the bathroom and I left it too long last month … so I had to cook a gourmet breakky for everyone on the weekend." She rolled her eyes in mock indignation. "Don't worry," she added with a grin, "it's never too harsh. I quite like cooking gourmet breakkies."

Over the next week, Gab was initiated into the rhythms of her new home. Of her housemates, Morgan was quiet, unobtrusive and beginning a degree in English literature. Steph, a second year

architecture student, was outspoken and had long, brightly deco-
rated fingernails—inconceivably impractical to Gab. And Freya was
Freya, with her long, thick plait of dark hair and her earnest, inquis-
itive eyes. She was always busy with sketching, costume design and
her next artistic piece.

Gab had landed.

CHAPTER 26

March

University. It loomed before her like a kingdom; Gab had come to find her place. She wasn't sure if she was arriving as the brave explorer or the bedraggled castaway. But there was possibility. She was here.

Classes began. Days were devoted to reading, learning and exploring ideas in areas Gab was most passionate about. She couldn't imagine anything better, though she missed Jack and Tony. Sharing chores with the other three girls in the apartment was a breeze for Gab, compared with what she'd been used to at home. And sharing the cooking! Gab couldn't believe her luck.

Unfortunately, she had developed nightmares. Gab would wake up shaking and drenched in sweat, thinking she'd heard Gina cry out—only realising after several moments that actually she was safe, far away, living in the city. The awful dreams left lingering imprints as her fears took shape in the strangest forms, revealing the terror that she'd hidden from herself.

After waking, Gab would lie there wondering, fearing what her mother was up to right at that moment; wondering whether Gina was safe or whether she was staring at her pills, fighting the desire to take them all at once. Then Gab felt wrought with guilt. She would resolve at 3am to go home and leave uni behind her; perhaps she would enrol in long-distance courses instead, like Mr. C. had suggested over a year ago. Then she'd think of Mr. C. and feel a spark of warmth just knowing he existed. She would hear him telling her that it was okay for her to be here, at uni, living her life. But the pain of longing and loss came with this too and confused her. Gab didn't know what it was or why it was so strong, and she didn't know how long she could bear it.

Things always looked different when the sun rose, and if the world of the night was a painful imposition on her health and her freedom, at least it receded into the distance and could be forgotten for a good twelve hours at a time … until the evening came round again, and Gab feared to meet herself and her hidden experiences in the world of her dreams.

* * *

Gina spent even longer meditating on her daughter's distance from her than Gab spent in worrying about her mother. Gina would sit brooding for hours, angry at Gab for leaving her behind, for reaching out for life, for succeeding in her ambition to go to university. It made Gina feel all the more a failure, though the way she explained it to herself was to say that Gab had deserted her. Besides, she felt unconsciously incompetent after years of having Gab meet her needs, and it was simply inconvenient to have to do things herself. Gina hated doing the grocery shopping. She hated leaving the house. She hated having to cook meals and often simply went without, although Tony was kind enough to bring extra meals down at least once a week.

"Come on, Gina," he said one evening, dropping off half a lasagne. "Be happy for the girl. She's making her own way in the world!"

"Yes Tony, but what kind of a way?" retorted Gina acerbically, standing at the front door and taking the meal Tony that handed her.

"Well, precisely the way that's right for her! She's clever, you know. She's studying something she loves!"

"I would have thought, Tony, that someone like you would understand the responsibilities of family."

"Ohhh, I see." Tony rolled his eyes and turned to leave. "Well, you just take care Gina. You don't be putting the guilts on Gab for going, you hear? She's got every right to go and live her life."

He walked back up the hill to his farmhouse. Sometimes he felt tempted to poison the lasagne, but he slapped himself on the metaphorical wrist whenever that thought snuck in.

CHAPTER 27

It was the third week of semester. Gab was walking across the courtyard on her way to her a lecture, eyeing off various food options for lunch on her way. That was something she loved about the city—the variety of cuisines on offer. Wattle Gully had a Chinese restaurant and pizza places of course—which, however, didn't do much to pass muster as Italian food. But here, there was so much more: Thai, South Indian, North Indian, Mongolian, Japanese, Singaporean, German, *real* Italian. She couldn't get enough of it and had decided to spend her weekends trying as many new flavours as she could afford. She often went alone, with a book; at other times, Freya came too.

Just as she got to the doors of the lecture theatre, Gab's phone rang. It was five minutes before the lecture was due to start, so Gab took out her phone. Mum. Again. Gina had developed a habit of calling at the most inconvenient times, but at least if there was a lecture starting soon, Gab could hang up with a decent excuse after a couple of minutes.

"Hi Mum," Gab answered, trying to sound happy to speak to Gina.

"Gab, I need you to tell me where you get those shortbread biscuit things. You know, the ones you used to buy with the shopping?" Not even a hello, Gab lamented. Straight to demands.

"Well, hi Mum to you too," said Gab sarcastically.

"No need to use that tone with me, young lady," reprimanded Gina. "Why don't you respect your mother?"

"Fine," Gab sighed. "Fine Mum. They're just from the bakery next to the supermarket. They usually have a buy-1-get-1-free deal."

"Good. Thanks darling," Gina's voice softened now that she had what she wanted. "I miss you!"

Gab sighed again. "Okay, thanks Mum. I've got a lecture now."

"Filling your head with all sorts of rubbish, no doubt."

"No, Mum," Gab's words were slow and deliberate. "It's really interesting actually. And important. You know, like about growing food and caring for the planet?" she added sarcastically.

"Alright darling, whatever you say." Gina's patronising tone was insufferable.

"Bye Mum." Gab hung up. But the lecture was ruined, because Gab spent it batting away the rising tide of indignation caused by her mother's idiotic insensitivity.

* * *

Freya was easy to talk to. Relaxed. She and Gab began catching up for lunch breaks between classes. The hours spent lying on the lawn together chatting, not chatting and just hanging out began to clock up. Freya's study was focused on performance design—so, there were always lots of theatre costumes and sets to be planned. Freya would describe her projects and Gab would suggest ideas; Freya would turn over in the grass, grab her backpack, dig out her pencil and start sketching them out. Freya had four sisters, lots of cousins and what Gab saw as successful, motivated parents—the opposite to Gab's life. Freya worked three evenings a week as an usher and she would tell Gab all about the latest shows and concerts, the troublesome people, the lighting schedules and the sets—and how she would design those things differently if they were up to her.

At first, Gab didn't tell Freya much about her home life yet; she was too embarrassed—she wanted to leave it behind. But Gina's text messages and phone calls kept coming, inevitably while they were eating lunch together or studying at home. The sinister, cold indifference that Gina had shown Gab since their fight when Gab first announced she was leaving had seemed like punishment to Gab—punishment for trying to live her own life. All Gina had said to Gab as she left were two words, and even those as if she regretted them being drawn out of her:

"Goodbye. Gabrielle."

But as soon as Gab had moved to Melbourne, the stony silence became a pestering, persistent lament, with constant warnings about the dangers of city life that, if not consciously *calculated* to heap guilt upon Gab, seemed to originate in that intention whether Gina was aware of it or not. Gina was not going to allow Gab to forget about her for a moment. And Gina was still asking Gab for money at least every three days, which was grating on Gab like nothing else. She really felt sorry for her mother, because some days Gina would tell Gab that there was no food in the house, that she had nothing to eat. And Gab wondered what the hell was happening with Gina's pension money, which was certainly not a large sum but—given the pittance Tony charged for rent of the granny flat—should certainly have seen her through with food for the fortnight. Gab's exasperation, instead of being so well hidden as in years before, was becoming palpable.

Every twenty dollars that Gab sent was like a piece of her soul being torn off, again and again and again. Not that her 'soul' was at all Scrooge-like when it came to money—quite the opposite. But it was the giving-in, the doing of something against her will, the indignity of being pestered until she caved in that was pulling one block after another out of the precarious block-tower of her life, making balance ever more precarious. Maybe she could persist forever, Gab thought. Wasn't generosity a good thing? Wasn't it more blessed to give than to receive? Gab couldn't work it out. At least Gina was far away.

But given the persistence of her phone calls and text messages, Gina wasn't ever really far away—not from Gab's mind nor concerns, even if she didn't have to make Gina's dinner every night. Life at university was better, but it was frustrating. Gab was free and not free. Plus, there were those nightmares.

CHAPTER 28

First week of April

One of Gina's strongest pulls on Gab was in blaming her for Jack's resistance to visiting home. This guilt-trip was deployed against Gab at least once a week. Since she had moved to the city in February, Jack had only been back to visit Gina twice and it was now April. Despite the complete narrow-mindedness of the deduction, Gina's conclusion was that this was Gab's fault. If Gab hadn't left, Jack would have wanted to be at home more often. Gina was sure that this was true. Maybe it was even Gab's fault that Jack had gone to live with Brian in the first place.

"Jack doesn't want to come here anymore!" Gina whined down the line. Gab was between classes, pacing back and forth along a shady avenue with her phone held a little away from her ear. "He only wants to stay at his dad's place!" Gina continued.

Gab didn't know what to say. They'd been through this a hundred times. She could understand entirely why Jack wanted to stay with his dad and why he didn't visit Gina. Jack's dad looked after him. Gina didn't. She was so relieved that Jack wasn't at home alone with Gina for any length of time.

Gina continued. "It's your fault you know! If you hadn't packed up and gone, things would be different. And I bet I can guess what you told Jack's social worker about me ... " Gina sounded like a moody, threatening child. Gab clenched her teeth. There was a screw tightening and tightening inside her, taking her mind in circles with it. She did not have the emotional energy for this ... again. Again. *Every day.* On Monday, it had been a dripping tap that Gina didn't know how to fix. On Tuesday, a case of bloating from eating Gina-didn't-know-what. On Wednesday, it was the unknown whereabouts of Gina's favourite bed linen. Yesterday, an ominous horoscope reading that had sent Gina into panic mode.

Gab didn't think Gina wanted Jack back at all; she was sure her mother was just hunting for reasons to lay guilt on her for moving out. Even so, as the frustration coursed through her, she felt guilty for it, and the tension hurt.

"I don't know what to say, Mum. I've given you my reasons, like, a million times. I can't help it if Jack doesn't want to come home!"

"But if you were here, he would come!" Gina whined. "He doesn't want to be at home with no one to play with."

Gab rolled her eyes and shook her head. Then she kicked a stone as hard as she could across the path.

"And," spoke Gina ominously, "I had a dream last night, Gabrielle. In it, your university turned into was a giant pit of quicksand, swallowing up the buildings and trees, and everyone who was there. Your whole apartment building was sucked in. You were there and you started sinking down, down, down. Gabrielle, you need to be careful. It was a warning, I'm sure of it. The city is not a safe place. University is not the right place for you."

When Gab thought it couldn't get any worse, it always got worse. She hung up.

"Bye, Mum!" she said with mock cheerfulness, and hung up. Then—"Blatant bloody coercion!" she yelled at her phone. She threw it into the garden.

Then she regretted that and ran to get it. But the anger remained.

CHAPTER 29

"Are you okay, Gab?" Freya touched her shoulder gently. Gab tightened her lips and shook head slightly, pulling her doona over her head.

"Did your mum call again?" Freya asked.

Gab nodded, and Freya sighed.

"That sucks," she said. She had watched Gab try to reason with her mother on the phone enough now to decide that she didn't envy Gab the task, nor the relationship.

"What's on tonight?" asked Gab, all of a sudden poking her head out from under the covers and looking at Freya. "With the others, I mean?"

"Not heaps. Steph and Dylan are organising something at his place."

"Are you going?"

"No, I hadn't planned to. Sounds like it'll be loud and over-crowded. Probably hectic," Freya predicted.

"Can we go?" Gab asked. "I want hectic."

"You do?" asked Freya, surprised. "I thought you didn't like that kind of thing."

"Not usually," replied Gab. She shrugged. "Just feel like something different. Don't care anymore."

"Okay," said Freya. "I don't mind."

Gab nodded. That was that.

* * *

Freya and Gab walked into the already-overcrowded Brunswick townhouse, owned by Dylan's parents. The sun was setting and the smell of jasmine battled with lingering smells of stale petroleum for ascendency. Gab wondered vaguely how Dylan was going to get away with this obnoxious event, given the non-space between neighbours. Then she remembered she didn't care about anything anymore, and she just wanted to forget—to forget there was ever anything like responsibility or guilt. It was anger today. Anger and apathy.

They knocked, and no one answered, so they opened the door. As they stepped over the threshold, Steph appeared on her way to the kitchen.

"Hey, you guys!" she shouted over the music; she came over to give them each a quick hug. "Gab!" Steph looked her up and down and Gab pretended not to notice. "You're wearing makeup! You're dressed up! You look great."

"Thanks," Gab looked aside.

"We've got food," said Freya. "Where do we put it?"

"Thanks guys! Just chuck it on the kitchen table." Steph gestured to a room on the right of the narrow passage. Gab thought she saw the wall pulse with heavy bass coming from around the corner. Just then a guy Gab vaguely recognised came and put his arms around Steph. It wasn't Dylan.

"Hey Stephie, who are your friends?" he grinned foolishly. Steph looked uncomfortable with this guy pressed against her, but she didn't push him away.

"Robbie! Are you pissed *already*?" she asked, semi-playfully.

"Nah, coursssse not," he said. Gab usually felt the urge to punch these sorts of guys in the face and tell them to get lost. But strangely today, she felt an odd pull of attraction. Robbie let go of Steph and came and stood between Freya and Gab.

"Ladies!" he said, offering them each an arm, "Let me take youuuu, to the ballroom!"

Steph grabbed the chips and dip from Freya and the pack of donuts from Gab.

"Go on girls," she said. "Have fun!"

The bass got louder as Robbie took Freya and Gab to the lounge. The furniture was against the walls, the curtains were closed, it was dark, and the fairy lights strung across the room set off an ambient glow. Bodies whirled and pulsed and pressed to a pervading beat. It was alluring. It was a place to forget yourself. Right now, Gab was all for it.

"You ladies want a drink?" yelled Robbie in Gab's ear. Gab nodded but Freya shook her head.

"No thanks," she yelled back.

"Okay, drink for one!" And Robbie ducked off to a table in the corner that was piled high with cheap alcohol.

"Hey Freya!" a couple of girls sitting on the couch hailed Freya.

"I might go sit with the girls a bit," Freya half motioned, half spoke to Gab. "Come if you want!"

Gab was about to nod, but then Robbie was there, handing her a colourful bottle and suddenly, his hand took hers and it was clear he was inviting her to dance. Gab shrugged.

"Have fun!" smiled Freya. She went over to the couch to join the girls she knew.

Yes. This. This was exactly what Gab needed. Robbie pulled her into the centre of the room and she just stood there, head back, arms down, letting the noise and the movement roll over her. It was so good. It was so empty. The layers and layers of complexity that always cloaked her simply melted away, and there was only darkness and bass and a weird tasting drink and Robbie.

CHAPTER 30

Gab was aware of the pounding headache before anything else. She raised her eyelids as slightly as possible. She was on the floor. Somewhere. A bedroom. Where was she again? Then she became aware of an arm draped over her ... a masculine arm covered in blonde hairs. Shock reared but was quelled quickly by the headache and the heaviness and the sense of relief that it was to be lying down somewhere—anywhere. Then she realised her jeans were scrunched up next to her head, which seemed odd, when she should have been wearing them ...

An intensely sick feeling filled her that was only partly due to the uncharacteristic amount of alcohol she had ingested the night before. But, as with all her feelings these days, it was soon accompanied by the opposite sensation, which was a sense of surrender. It was nothingness and numbness. Apathy. Who cared? She was sick of monitoring her every move with way too much attention. She was sick of regulating everything she said and everything she did, and she wasn't responsible for Jack anymore. She was free. She could do what she wanted. And her mum was *not* there. Gab was an adult. It was an intoxicating realisation—and it wasn't an intoxication that would land her with a throbbing headache.

As soon as her eyes had semi-adjusted to the light, Gab moved Robbie's arm and rolled over. A sheet was tangled around their legs and Robbie was in his boxer shorts. Gab looked for a moment at him, half mesmerised by his difference to herself, and part afraid. What exactly had happened? She had no idea, but she knew that the evidence pointed to something not quite in line with her life plan. She was afraid to think about it. She didn't want to know. She pulled her jeans on. Her phone was still in her jean's pocket. Thank God. 5:17am. Where was Freya? The last thing she remembered was seeing her with a bunch of her friends, moving out into the court-yard so they didn't have to yell so loudly over the music.

Gab padded down the stairs that presented themselves as she left the bedroom and found her way back to the lounge. People were strewn about on the floor and on couches, but she couldn't see Freya. *Oh well*, she thought. It was time to go home.

CHAPTER 31

April

It had been three weeks since the party and Gab hadn't seen or heard from Robbie since. She couldn't decide whether she felt relief or despair at this, though she imagined she'd drop dead with embarrassment if she actually had to talk to him again. She wanted to leave that party well and truly behind her. Last week, Steph had mentioned that Robbie was a ring-in friend of Dylan's who lived in Camberwell and was doing an Arts degree. She'd looked at Gab strangely when she'd said that. Gab tried to block it out; she was attempting to categorise Robbie as chimera. A haze. Someone who didn't really exist. But … she couldn't help wondering, fearing, what had happened that night.

"He's got a girlfriend," said Steph knowingly, as they sat around eating breakfast one autumnal morning. Gab's stomach dropped. "But she wasn't at Dylan's party."

Gab looked down into her cereal, her head spinning. *Just. Great.* she thought. This was a horror. This wasn't her. Had she cheated on someone without even knowing it?

Freya put a hand on her arm. "It's his responsibility, not yours," she said.

"I feel sick," said Gab.

"So would I, if I'd slept with Robbie!" Steph scoffed, finally saying what she'd been tempted to say for the last three weeks.

"No, I mean, I really feel sick," said Gab, suddenly too ill to react to Steph's jibe. "I'm going back to bed".

Relief was waiting for her under the covers. She closed her eyes and stayed there for an hour, drifting between sleep and vague questions about her life and where it was going. Why always contradictory feelings? Freedom and guilt; liberation and emptiness; anger and apathy. As she dozed, her dreams were uncomfortable and grotesque; she was tied up in a huge knot in one of them, and in another, her teeth were long and contorted and growing all wrong. She had to spit them out.

That evening, she couldn't bare the smell of dinner as she cooked and had to pinch her nose shut as she stirred the stir fry with satay sauce. It got right up into her head, clouded her brain, sickened her stomach. She tried to eat some but ran to the bathroom moments later to bring it all up again, hoping desperately that she'd feel better in the morning.

She didn't. She woke on Monday with a spinning head, dreading class. She couldn't eat breakfast, so she shoved all her books in her backpack and went for a walk instead. *Maybe a fruit smoothie'll do the trick,* she thought. She picked one up from *So Smoothie* and wandered towards her favourite spot in the park across from their apartment. She took tiny sips of smoothie that sort-of helped wash away the disgusting feeling she couldn't shake. She lay down on the grass and closed her eyes.

"So. Tired," she thought. "So tired of everything ... uni is bloody exhausting. Life is exhausting!".

Suddenly she opened her eyes, and the sun was somewhere different. Gab checked her watch. 10:03am. She'd slept for an hour on the lawn, and class was starting now! She grabbed her bag and stood up—but way too quickly, and had to sit down again so that she didn't pass out. *I should really drink more water*, she thought.

Gab sat in *Foundations of Ag. Science*, not really listening—which was uncharacteristic, because she generally felt engaged in this class, and the end of semester was looming. She tapped her pen on her knee, doodled asymmetrical patterns in her notebook, and tried to pretend that life was simple. Then she was thinking of Mr. Cheng; he hadn't crossed her mind for a while. She wondered what he was up to and how his Year 12 Maths class was going. Maybe she should call him. She wanted to, a bit. But for some reason, the thought of it made her palms sweaty.

By next Monday, she was still sick. Freya came into her bedroom in the morning.

"You still sick, honey?"

"Mmm-hmm," came a muffled voice. It was so quiet Freya barely heard it. She came and sat on the bed.

"Gab? Do you want to talk?"

Gab shook her head.

"Heard anything from your mum lately?"

Gab turned over so that her face wasn't buried in the pillow. "I've been ignoring her. She's been texting non-stop." She reached for her phone, unlocked it and thrust it towards Freya. "Take a look if you want."

"Do you want me to?"

"Yeah."

The latest message from Gina read: *My darling Gabrielle, my angel, sent from above. Don't forget me while your busy. Children who honor there parents are blessed. Come home soon. Its too quiet without you and I need help with shopping. Love Mum xx*

There were about ten more from the last three days of a similar vibe.

"Ugh. How do you deal with this?" asked Freya. Gab shrugged.

"It's my mum. Just do."

"It sounds backwards to me," observed Freya.

"How so?" asked Gab, sitting up very slowly.

"You're the parent, the responsible one who looks after her, and calms her down when she's anxious. And she's the kid, relying on you for everything," Freya said.

"Yeah. So true," said Gab. "But after all these years, I haven't managed to fix things, and I don't know why."

"Because it's not your job, Gab," Freya said, gently.

"Wish I had sisters like yours," said Gab shyly.

"Well, seeing as there are four of us already, another won't hurt. You can be sister number five." Freya smiled. "Come back and stay with us sometime. If you can handle a house of six people, two dogs, four guinea pigs and homing pigeons."

"Homing pigeons? What the? Are they a real thing?"

"Yeah," grinned Freya. "They're my dad's. He's super keen on them."

"What! Your Dad sounds cool. How old are your sisters again?"

"Priya's twenty-three, Indira's seventeen and Lena's fifteen," said Freya, smoothing out the bottom edges of Gab's doona. "My dad has Scandinavian and Scottish heritage," she continued, "and my mum's Indian."

"Wow! How did they meet?" Gab's curiosity was clouding out her nausea.

"Ha, they met at an art gallery in Berlin."

"What! And ... your mum's a doctor, right?" This was good medicine.

"Yes, with endless energy. We can't keep up with her!"

"And your dad?"

"He's a primary school teacher. His favourite time of the year is when he takes his homing pigeons into school to show his Grade Sixes. It's always during their module on technology." Freya laughed. "Mum says he likes it better than Christmas."

Gab was incredulous, busily piecing together such an unfamiliar family scenario. Freya's tone suggested happy camaraderie.

Freya laughed again and began unplaiting and re-plaiting her dark hair. "Dad's students always think he's pretty cool. They aren't quite old enough to scoff at his dagginess yet, but we give him crap all the time."

"Does he mind?"

"Nah, he's a good sport. He says, in a house of five women, he gave up on trying to win arguments years ago!"

Gab smirked.

The girls were quiet for a moment.

"Do you … ever see your dad?" asked Freya, her voice faltering.

Gab shook her head and shrugged. "No, never met him. Don't even know his name. Doesn't bother me mostly. You can't miss what you never had." And, although Gab had believed that until now, a sudden pang stabbed a hole underneath that belief and it slipped away. It was gone before she'd finished speaking the words.

"I had a great teacher in Grade Six actually," she added, trying to patch up the hole just a little bit. "Mr. Cheng. He didn't have homing pigeons but he was cool. Then he started teaching maths at high school and … oh … crap!"

Gab jumped up from the bed, clapped her hand over her mouth and ran for the bathroom. Freya heard retching sounds and felt sorry for her friend; she worried about these signs of unease. Gab hadn't been eating much. She'd been sleeping a lot and was quieter than usual. Freya's sister Indira had struggled with food and had teetered on the edge of an eating disorder. Freya wondered if she should call her mum for advice about Gab.

First week of May

I'm just going to do it, thought Gab, as she crossed the campus between classes. After all, Mr. C. had given her his number when she'd left and had invited her to call anytime. Of course, she hadn't. It felt like crossing some invisible boundary. Still, Gab wasn't the same person as she had been only three months before. So she dialled, not even thinking that it was during school hours and that Mr. Cheng would be teaching—until she got his voicemail. It caught her off-guard and she hung up quickly.

* * *

"Gab, I'm worried about you. You've been feeling sick for a month," Freya said.

"Yeah," said Gab, sitting on her bed in her pyjamas and hugging her knees to her chest. "It sucks. I hate it."

"Do you think maybe ... Is it worth going to the doctor?" asked Freya.

"Don't like doctors," muttered Gab, breathing in slowly through her nose, and trying to ignore the acrid taste of bile seeping up the back of her throat. Then she realised what she'd said. "I mean, ...

sorry Freya. I don't have anything against doctors. I just don't like *going* to them."

"Don't you?" asked Freya. Gab shook her head.

"Mum's a hypochondriac," she explained. "She's always afraid of what's happening in her own body. It's like it's a stranger to her. She takes twenty pills every morning, calls out for painkillers at the drop of a hat, and I've lost hours of my life listening to detailed weather reports on the state of her bowels."

Freya could't help grinning at Gab's narrative flair.

"Plus," added Gab, "why would I want to go tell a stranger such personal things? And why would I want them to touch me?" The thought of telling someone how she was feeling and then being treated flippantly or patronisingly squeezed Gab into a tiny place. Freya wanted to explain why it might be a good idea after all but then caught herself. Instead, she said,

"I know what you mean. But, if you like, I could take you to see my mum at her clinic? I know you haven't met her before," she added quickly, "but you and I get on pretty well—and you're adopted as an extra sister now, remember?"

Gab thought about it. She didn't mind the idea of talking to Freya's mum so much actually. And, she had been curious for a while about meeting her.

"I guess that sounds okay," agreed Gab. "I'll see your mum ... if ... she won't mind? Will she?"

"Course she won't," Freya reassured her. She hid her relief well, but Gab wouldn't have noticed it anyhow—because she felt relieved herself.

CHAPTER 34

"Can you ..." began Gab under her breath. But then she stopped and waves of hot tingles flashed through her.

"Pardon?" asked Freya.

"Doesn't matter," mumbled Gab. They sat in a medical clinic waiting room in Burwood. This was the practice where Freya's mum, Saanvi, worked. Freya had come with Gab for moral support—and partly so that Gab didn't get lost or pike. Now Gab was waiting to go in for her appointment and fear took shape like bony fingers sitting ominously around her neck. *What if something is really wrong?* she thought. *What if I'm anorexic? Or what if I've picked up some weird parasite from the foods I've eaten? What if I've got cancer?* Life had been flat and colourless for weeks. She had been vomiting every day and couldn't stand the sight of food. *What if my stupid weirdo life is catching up with me? What if Mum was right and I should have stayed home?* The thoughts were lead heavy, landing with a weight that shot her up high into the ether, disconnected from everything around her.

"Gabrielle Lander?"

A petite woman with black plaited hair streaked grey called Gab's name with a smile. Gab recognised the smile at once. She stood up. Then she turned back to Freya and said breathlessly,

"Can-you-come-in-with-me-please?"

"Of course," said Freya, not missing a beat. She had wanted to offer but didn't want to intrude, especially when Gab was already so self-conscious.

Dr. Saanvi Ashwanti led the girls to a small room at the end of the passageway.

"Come in, girls," she motioned, with an almost imperceptible tilt of her head. Something about her was dignified, Gab thought. Having Freya come in with a ragamuffin misfit didn't seem to rattle her in the least; at least, Gab felt like a ragamuffin misfit.

"Sit down, please," motioned Saanvi, as the girls entered the consultation room. "I'm Saanvi. What can I do for you, Gabrielle?"

Gab looked down at her fingers and played with the rip in her jeans. "I haven't been feeling well," she said after a moment, and she felt seven years old and completely stupid.

"I'm sorry to hear that, dear," said Saanvi, and Gab had heard that tone of voice before too. "What are your symptoms? What is bothering you?"

"Um ... I feel nauseous a lot. Mostly in the mornings, and I don't want to get out of bed. And I ... I can't be bothered with anything. It's been like this for about a month." She feared the consequences of admitting this. Would they send her to hospital? "Do you think I have depression?" she burst out suddenly, and for the first time, she looked up to meet the doctor's gaze. "My mum does," Gab continued quickly, "she's had it for years, I think. Maybe I've got it too."

"There are genetic factors involved in depression, of course," said Dr. Saanvi slowly, "but there's generally a lot more to it than that. You said you have been feeling nauseous? Is that your main complaint?"

"Um, yes I think so," said Gab. "But maybe it's anxiety. I've read that anxiety can cause nausea. Can anxiety make you vomit?"

"Have you been vomiting, too?" asked Saanvi gently.

Gab nodded. "What about anorexia?" she whispered. "I've been losing weight." She subconsciously pinched her belly between her fingers. Saanvi could see the profuse anxiety, but she wasn't sure it was the whole story.

"Gabrielle, would it be alright if I gave you a check-up? I'd like to look at a few things, like your eyes and ears, and check your heartbeat."

"Um, okay," agreed Gab nervously. "What do I have to do?"

"You just relax, dear. First, let me check your eyes." After checking Gab's furtive eyes, more to distract Gab from her nervous train of thought than anything, Saanvi checked her throat, her lungs and heartbeat, and her blood pressure. Gab was still fidgety, nervy, but the initial dysphoria was wearing off. Saanvi sat down to her computer.

"When was your last checkup, Gabrielle?" she asked.

Gab shrugged. "Maybe when I was six?" she guessed. Freya's eyes widened.

"That's a while, dear," said Saanvi stoically. "Have you been in good health?"

Gab shrugged again. "I guess so. I mean, I never think about it." Then she added, "My mum goes to the doctor a lot. But I'm not like her." Saanvi typed a few more notes and then turned to Gab.

"Gabrielle," she said softly, "you said you've felt nauseous and you've been vomiting. You haven't wanted to get out of bed. And you said you 'can't be bothered'. Do you mean, you've been feeling tired? Lacking energy?"

"Yes," said Gab, "that's right. So tired, Dr. Saanvi! I've been napping in the day and falling asleep in class."

Saanvi nodded.

"Anything else? Have your periods been normal?"

Gab frowned and looked at Freya instinctively. Again, she shrugged.

"I don't know. I don't really keep track." Something in her mind ticked over, even as she fought to stop it. And Freya knew then. She had thought of it earlier but had figured, and hoped, it was way too unlikely.

"Gabrielle, I'm going to ask you a very personal question, and I'm sorry if it feels intrusive. It will help me to help you as best I can, okay?"

Gab shrugged ... again ... and nodded. Saanvi proceeded.

"Gabrielle, do you think there's any chance you might be pregnant? Have you engaged in unprotected sex lately?"

Suddenly, Gab didn't feel anything. She was numb. She was watching the scene from outside her own body, as if the story wasn't her own, and she heard Dr. Saanvi's voice as if in echoes. She didn't answer.

"I think the best thing," said Saanvi carefully, after a moment, "is for me to send you for a blood test, Gabrielle. That will help us figure out what is going on."

Gab nodded mechanically. Saanvi printed out the slip, and just like that, Gab tumbled around a bend in the road that she never, not in a million years, would have guessed was coming.

CHAPTER 35

Doctor appointment + 6 hours

"Gab?" called Freya quietly. "Can I come in?" There was no response. She tiptoed quietly into Gab's dark room. It was evening now. Gab had not spoken a word on the tram ride back to their apartment, nor had she emerged for dinner. Shockwave after shockwave echoed through her body with varying intensities; they jolted her mind with an unassimilable new reality every time she began to relax. It couldn't be real.

Freya reached the bed where Gab lay facing out the window; Gab had not bothered to draw the curtains. City lights winked at them, a static scene seemingly unchanged by any such news that was enough to throw a single human being into a spiral of existential confusion. Then Freya laid a hand on Gab's shoulder, and a muffled and unexpected sob half-escaped Gab before she could stop it. Having only half-escaped, it was more like a snort, and both girls laughed involuntarily. But having now unlocked a half-sob and a laugh, there was no going back; further sobs escaped.

Freya slipped into bed next to Gab, as naturally and unobtrusively as a girl with three sisters knows how to do. But for Gab, such presence was entirely new. When was the last time she had been able to rest on another person? When was the last time someone had positioned themselves so close, so present, so willing to absorb her own tumult? What did it mean when another person felt so comfortable, so confident in themselves, that they could slip under the covers, wrap their arms around you, and share your grief without reservation? It was strange. Freya was mediating Gab's grief.

CHAPTER 36

Doctor appointment + 1 day (AM)

The next morning dawned grey and misty; reality hit Gab like a ton of bricks. She felt her innards drain out, out of the soles of her feet, and she was wobbly and empty. She also felt nauseous. And she felt warm, because Freya's back was pressed against hers.

Freya felt Gab stir. She had woken early; she had been thinking.

"Gab?" she said. "Do you want some crackers? They're meant to help with nausea." Freya had been doing some early morning research. Gab shrugged and Freya got up and went to the kitchen. She dug out a box of crackers from the pantry. She also made a peppermint tea for each of them. When she returned to Gab's room, her friend was retching into an empty yoghurt tub as if her life depended on it. The gut-wrenching episode over, Gab took a cracker and made mouse-sized nibbles around its edges.

"Gab," began Freya, "if you don't want to wait for the blood test results, you could get a test from the pharmacy." Thankfully, Freya hadn't mentioned the p-word. Gab nodded and nibbled.

"The other thing is," said Freya, "your body is your body. If the test comes back positive, you still have options."

* * *

Gab was lost. So many others had been in this situation before; countless others, like grains of sand on the seashore. But she couldn't absorb all the lessons of history simply by being contemporary; the fresh immediacy of personal implication stung with a vengeance.

She was by turns disbelieving, angry, horrendously sad, as though she had lost something and she didn't know what. And she felt caught in a web of dilemmas. Home. Money. Support. Uni. Where would any of it come from? And ... a baby. A real one. It was all too bizarre.

There was so much Gab had to muster for herself; so much inventing, because she had no helpful blueprint for what happened next. Her care of Jack gave her some practical experience, but this was different. This was her own child. This was her whole identity and the trajectory of her life. It was her body. Her image. Her self-understanding, her place in the world.

She felt like a wanderer, an exile, with concerns different to those of her peers—and that had always been the way. It was those hard edges of lack that she continually brushed up against. They shaped a certain view of life. Others seemed to have a buffer; she didn't begrudge them that. But she didn't enjoy the knowledge that, when the cookie of life had crumbled, she'd seemed to get a particularly meagre helping. She knew others were worse off, of course, so she felt guilty for admitting to any sense of lack. But somehow recognising that her crumbs were meagre made her more determined. Was it possible to make something out of not-much? Was it possible to make crumbs somehow into a banquet, or deficiency into some kind of advantage? She didn't know.

CHAPTER 37

Doctor appointment + 1 day (PM)

Gab didn't say anything. She just pulled on a hoodie, covered as much of her face as she could, slipped her purse into her pocket and walked to the nearest pharmacy. It was an hour before closing time.

She had never been into this shop. The advantage of that was that they didn't know her; the downside was that she didn't know where anything was and had to ask one of the shop assistants for help.

"Where abouts are your pregnancy tests?" she muttered, as quietly as she could. It was the first time she had said the word *pregnancy*, and it tasted strange in her mouth. The shop assistant led her to the relevant aisle. Gab's head spun as she looked at shelves and shelves of packaged fate. She didn't know the first thing about pregnancy tests. Why should she choose one over any other? She kicked herself for not having thought of this earlier.

She tried to talk quietly when she asked the shop assistant which she should choose, but the girl, probably about fifteen, was jolly and exuberant. It seemed absurd to be given advice on pregnancy tests by a fifteen-year-old who did not look like the kind of girl who had used one before—but then, Gab suddenly realised that she was becoming the kind of person lots of people made presumptions about, and it was only fair and feeling not to make similar presumptions about others. Who knew what this girl had or hadn't been through? This all flickered through Gab's mind in wordless forms, while the girl explained the difference between the EarlyTest and the MummaNew. A decision felt impossible in that moment, so Gab let the shop girl choose, paid for the test, shoved it in her pocket and walked home.

* * *

Gab had to pee on the stick while sitting on the toilet. Then the stick would tell her whether she was pregnant or not. Two lines, pregnant. One line, probably not. *What an idyllic place to learn of my fate*, thought Gab wryly. She didn't want to take the test at home in the apartment where the others would be around. She went to her most-used block of uni toilets instead, locked herself in one of the many empty cubicles and got out the test. She read the instructions from top to bottom. She took the stick out of its plastic wrapping and tried to position its tip in the predicted wee-stream. She did hit the stick a bit, but she also got her hand. She would have recoiled, but she was too focused on the test. No turning back now. Hopefully enough wee had landed where it was meant to.

Gab sat, elbows on knees, pants around ankles, staring at the little white stick she was holding in both hands. She watched the stream of moisture gradually seep up, up the indicator strip until it reached the point where the lines were meant to appear. Her heart began to thump. One line. The moisture seeped up further. No second line. Not immediately. But then, faintly, faintly it began to show. It became stronger and unarguable in its prominence. Two lines. Gab's heart skipped a beat. But then she just felt dazed, numb. Maybe it was wrong? These things couldn't always be accurate. Better try another one, to be sure. Gab gingerly laid the first test down on the tiled floor by her shoe. She took the box out of her front hoodie pocket and opened up a second test. Then she remembered about the bladder factor, but thankfully, there was a little dribble that eked out onto the stick ... and onto her hand, again. She rolled her eyes, wiped her hand with some fresh toilet paper, and held the stick up to watch the moisture run up.

Two lines, again. Unmistakable. This was it. She dropped the second test on the floor and let her head sink into her hands. But just as she did so, she remembered she'd just peed on her hand ... twice. So she wiped, pulled up her pants, gathered her bits and pieces together and flushed the toilet. Then she proceeded to the basins to clean herself up, in the knowledge that she'd seen two lines ... twice.

CHAPTER 38

Having finished in the bathroom, all Gab could do was walk. She had to walk and walk and walk, and if there were people around her, she had no idea. Gab walked past old buildings, past shops, over crossings, through parks, under trees. This thing inside her ... this growing mass of cells that perhaps already had a beating heart ... it was such an entirely disproportionate, preposterous outcome to one evening, one hour, maybe even one minute completely out of beat with the rest of Gab's existence. It was living evidence of actions Gab could not even integrate into her own self-understanding. She couldn't accept what she had done, couldn't even believe it; it was like trying to absorb a solid object through her skin. And yet this was living proof. What should she do? What could she do?

This whole situation could be solved with one decision. She turned it over and over in her mind. But something in her was resisting. The voices in her head spoke loudly.

It will be too much. You can't manage it.

That's the end of uni. No career, no future.

You are not old enough to have a baby!

Wow, you fell pregnant to someone you don't even know?

And the worst one: *Like mother, like daughter.*

Gab didn't need to encounter other peoples' judgmental sentiments, uninformed incredulity or discomfort with her situation to hear these pronouncements. She didn't need them, because all those judgments arose within herself. She knew what others might say; she knew the looks she'd get. And there was that intractable question about Robbie. The thought of telling him and the imagined implications of what might follow were unendurable. As she walked, the urges she felt to end her life and escape the shame of it all became so awful, so heavy, that all she could do was put one foot in front of the other. But her soul was dragging, falling down into the concrete. It just wasn't possible for her to cope with this. If Robbie was single, maybe it would be different. Maybe not. The thought of being shackled to another person through a child—of being roped into relationally with someone she had hardly met and didn't know—that was absurd enough.

As the sun began to set, Gab realised that she needed to turn around and walk home. As she made her way past a row of townhouses, she heard a baby crying, jolting her to awareness. She stopped to listen. One decision. One afternoon, and no one would know. That would be it; it would be gone, all evidence, all change. Her path restored.

The baby cried on and on. The sound tugged at her heart strings, seeming to last forever. Where were the child's parents? Who was going to comfort and look after it? Gab couldn't bear it. Her hand went instinctively to her abdomen. Then, the baby stopped crying. Had it been comforted? She hoped so. In fact, the baby had been crying only as long as it might have taken anyone to walk from downstairs to the upper floor, but to Gab it had felt like forever.

She shook her head and continued. Her mother would have said it was a sign, but she was doing everything she could not to think of her mother right now; not to think about following in her mother's footsteps. That was the worst thought of all. And yet, to eradicate this growing mass of cells—did she want that? What would be worse —having her life turned upside down by becoming a single mother at nineteen? Or continuing things as they were while knowing she *could* have had something entirely new, unexpected—her own child —and that she had chosen not to? Would she spend her life wondering about this almost-child? Wishing she'd been able to meet it? It seemed obvious that having her life turned upside down by a baby was by far the worse option; but something in still resisted.

What the hell would she do with it? Where would she live? Could she afford it? Would she have to move back home again, now that she had tasted freedom? It was unimaginable; she couldn't go back— she just couldn't. Her sanity, her wellbeing, her ability to cope with life was at stake. She couldn't have Gina looking over her shoulder constantly, telling her what to do or freaking out all the time.

Gab was halfway back to the apartment when she thought of Freya. And then she thought of Saanvi. And she felt a spark of warmth, just a tiny one. She felt that in the few moments of time she had witnessed mother and daughter together, she had seen something she wanted. Something comfortable; something like home. She thought of Freya's family. Things didn't *have* to be what Gab had always known. There might be alternatives.

Gab thought too of working with Tony on the farm and of his teaching her to drive. She thought of Mr. C and how it felt when he'd said he was proud of her. She knew she held her head high now through others' belief in her—belief that came even before she was ready to genuinely believe it herself. This wasn't a fake overcompensation for insecurity. This was genuine, growing confidence.

"You've got as much right to be out there, living your life, as anyone," Mr. C had told her once. "And as much right to be happy, too."

Yes. She did. Why should she miss out?

The problem was, it felt like she would be missing out either way: baby or no-baby.

CHAPTER 39

Doctor appointment + 2 days

Saanvi herself phoned Gab to tell her that the blood test results had arrived. She invited Gab to come in the next day; she wanted to give her the results in person.

"I took a pregnancy test, Dr. Saanvi," Gab told her, sitting on her bed in her room with the door closed and talking as quietly as possible.

"Oh, yes?"

"Yes ... um, Freya suggested it. And, I just wanted to know."

"Yes, of course. I understand. And?"

"And it showed two lines. And ... and I realised I hadn't had my period since before the party where ... Anyway, I haven't had it for more than five weeks now. So, I guess that's that."

"Okay, dear," said Saanvi. "Yes. The blood test also showed hormone levels that indicate that you are pregnant. Five weeks." Even though Gab knew, even though she had just said it, a wave of shock crashed over her again.

"Are you alright, dear?" asked Saanvi. "I'd like you to come in and see me tomorrow, if you're able. We can discuss your options and I can give you a further check-up."

"Alright," agreed Gab.

They said goodbye and Gab lay on her bed, a million things whirring through her mind. She couldn't shut her mind up—one voice after another after another, decrying her stupidity, voicing her disbelief, lamenting the dead end her life would become, freaking out at the impossibility of taking even one step forward. The problems were too much. She grabbed her head with her hands.

"STOP!" she yelled, and then realised she had said it aloud and coloured with embarrassment, because Freya was in the lounge room studying.

Gab got up quickly.

"You okay?" asked Freya as Gab walked into the lounge. Gab shook her head and sat down on the couch, her head in her hands.

"Your mum called," said Gab.

"With the results?"

"Yes."

Freya didn't ask. She just sat there next to Gab in heavy silence. Then Gab remembered the baby she'd heard crying yesterday when she'd been out walking. It stirred a memory that the fingers of her consciousness reached out to grasp.

"A girl at my school got pregnant in Year 11," said Gab quietly, not looking at Freya. "The doctor assumed she'd get rid of it. He basically pushed her to do it, she told us later. But she wanted the baby."

"What happened?" asked Freya quietly, wondering where this was going.

"She kept it," said Gab. "And she came back to school after a year."

"That's so brave," said Freya.

"I know," said Gab. "We couldn't believe she did it." She was quiet for a minute. "You know Freya, I thought it was really cool. She knew what she wanted and she stuck with it. She made it work." Freya nodded, still wondering where this was leading.

"You know what really sucks?" asked Gab, suddenly becoming animated. "What are the chances, Freya? I mean, *what the hell*?"

"I know," agreed Freya. "I can't believe it."

"I don't even know what happened. I don't know what I agreed to. I don't even know what I did." Gab paused. "This is going to haunt me forever, isn't it?"

"Maybe." Freya couldn't pretend it was less difficult than it was.

"I'm going to see your mum tomorrow," said Gab.

"Do you want me to come?" Freya asked.

"Yes please, to help me get there. And maybe to come in with me again?" Gab was a seasoned professional at going things alone emotionally, of bottling up what life was offering and carrying it along with her without saying much about it. But this companionship had some kind of captivating quality, and now that Gab had had a taste of what it was like to be accompanied by a friend in an awful situation, she was timidly keen for more.

CHAPTER 40

The next day, Gab went to visit Saanvi at her clinic again.

Saanvi talked Gab through her options: how she might go about terminating the pregnancy and conversely, what would happen next if she decided to continue with it. She would be booked into the prenatal clinic at the hospital, just around the corner from their apartment block and would continue with check-ups there. Saanvi gave Gab various brochures and information booklets to take with her and read through. At some points in the conversation, Gab thought she had fully made up her mind to keep the baby; then, the uncertainty of it all came crashing down over her and she felt lost in the dark, surrounded by obstacles and hazards she couldn't see. There was no way she could keep it. No way. But Saanvi reassured her that she didn't have to decide straight away. She had time.

As they left the doctors surgery, Gab's mind felt so full it was going to explode, and she wasn't sure for how long she could endure the tension. Indecision was painful and Gab was tossed this way and that, with the full weight of her emotions. Termination meant hiding her mistake. A baby was sure to lead to others' judgment. It would change everything.

* * *

The next week of classes was a complete blur, as Gab continued to feel disgustingly nauseated every day. Looming exams would wait for no one, or rather, would continue to come closer despite the fact that all this made it impossible for Gab to even think about studying. What had once become a life-giving escape for Gab was no longer that, and it was all she could do to scrape through her essential tasks. This was so disappointing to Gab, the high achiever, that it sent her into an emotional spin. She couldn't stop thinking of Mr. C. and what he would say if he knew she was bombing out ... and why. She'd let him down. And what about Tony? He had been so excited for her too, so supportive. And if he knew ...

She had cut off those whose good opinions she cared most about. Their faith in her had given her so much strength, and she was sure she'd lose it all once they found out what she'd done and where she'd landed. She had nothing left.

CHAPTER 41

Late June, exams
Early July, mid-semester break

Exams came and went. Gab passed, but not well. The nausea finally began to relent when she was fifteen weeks pregnant, but she still hadn't made up her mind about what to do next. She had until twenty-four weeks of pregnancy to easily access a termination, and she was putting off the final decision, fluctuating between a sense of just waiting to see what was around the corner, and denying the whole situation entirely, pretending it wasn't there.

Over the mid-semester break, Freya invited Gab to come and stay with her family. Gab agreed timidly. Did they all know about the pregnancy? She felt self-conscious.

"Don't worry," said Freya. "Mum would never tell them. She's very strict about things like confidentiality and boundaries. In fact, she'll probably tell you specifically when you come home that she's not your doctor when we're there! She's embarrassing like that. Embarrassing, but good," she added.

The next day the girls took the tram back to Freya's family home. They arrived and walked in the backdoor, Gab with her pillow and backpack. Saanvi greeted them both with a hug, and—as Freya had predicted—said to Gab:

"When we're here, Gab, I'm just Saanvi, okay? Not doctor." She smiled. "You can call me Aunty, or Saanvi, or Freya's Mum ... whatever you like."

"How about *Mum*—like everyone else does around here!" said Freya. "And hi Mum!" Freya went and gave her a hug, which was a very different scenario to their interaction at the doctor's clinic. Gab thought Freya was joking about having her call Saanvi *Mum*, but Saanvi absorbed it naturally and said, "Yes, of course. Whatever you prefer."

"My two best friends in high school called my parents Mum and Dad," explained Freya, when she saw Gab's surprise. "Doesn't hurt to borrow someone else's parents every now and then!"

"What are your parents' names?" asked Saanvi to Gab.

"Oh, just Gina," said Gab. "My mum's name is Gina. Yeah, she's a bit of a weird one."

Saanvi recalled that first appointment, when Gab had expressed fear about being like her mother. Despite the work-home boundary line, Saanvi couldn't *not* carry this knowledge with her. But she held it carefully, observing with gentle understanding.

"I haven't told my Mum," Gab blurted out suddenly. Then she felt like an idiot. She didn't specify what exactly she hadn't told her mum, but both Freya and Saanvi knew.

"There's time," said Saanvi, patting Gab's hand.

Gab still had no idea how to tell Gina. It seemed like the logical thing to do, the normal thing, to tell her mum she was having a baby. If she was Freya—well, maybe it wouldn't have been easy, not in those circumstances, but she couldn't imagine Saanvi being anything but helpful and supportive. Perhaps in her grief, Gab's perception of Freya and Saanvi's relationship was oversimplified or romanticised. But nothing at all seemed simple about her relationship with Gina—except that Gina needed Gab's help simply to get by. Maybe Gina wasn't malicious. She was just ... empty. Fearful.

Pretentious. Under-resourced. But what did that mean for Gab? Was it her burden to bear?

"Come on Gab, let me show you round!" said Freya, taking Gab's bag and pillow from her. "And I'll introduce you to the sisters. Who's home, Mum?" she asked, as she turned down the passageway, beckoning Gab after her.

"Just the young ones," Saanvi called after her.

The house was big but not astoundingly so for a house of six, plus pets. Wood panelling lined the walls and the ceiling downstairs, and Freya led Gab down the end of the passageway to a timber staircase.

"Up here," she said, and they walked up the stairs to an open loft, with two beds, desks and lots of photos on the walls. "I share with Priya," explained Freya. "So she gets the room to herself while I'm gone. The younger girls share a room downstairs."

"What does Priya do?" asked Gab, scanning Priya's desk, her bed, the photos on her wall.

"She's studying education," said Freya, "to teach primary school like Dad."

"Where are the homing pigeons?" asked Gab, suddenly remembering.

"Ah! I'll introduce you to them later," laughed Freya. "Just don't ask Dad about them. He'll give you a history of the homing pigeon and you'll never escape." She winked. Then she said, "You can sleep in my bed and I'll grab a lilo for the floor." Freya threw Gab's pillow onto her bed and laid the bag on the floor next to it.

"Oh no," said Gab, "keep your bed! I'll use the lilo."

"No way! And you can't win an argument with me on home turf, Gabby!" said Freya, joking but firm, flicking her long black plait over her shoulder with a grin. "The bed's yours. Besides, I like the lilo. Reminds me of happy camping days."

Gab was silently inspecting the shelf above Freya's bed with its various trinkets, books and photos. Gab noticed a canister of brushes and trays of watercolour paint; a photo of Freya and her family in front of the Taj Mahal; an eclectic mix of books—Enid Blyton sat with Arundhati Roy and Nelson Mandela; Jane Austen leant up against Gertrude Stein. There was a beautiful wooden box, carved with elephants, and a collection of delicate, clay-sculpted dancers that Gab assumed had been shaped and painted by Freya.

"Wait there," said Freya, and she ran downstairs to a cupboard in the hallway, and came back up again a moment later, lugging an inflatable mat and a pump.

"Get comfy then!" said Freya, motioning to a beanbag and the bed. Gab sat down gingerly on the bed. "You okay Gab?" asked Freya, more quietly. Gab nodded.

"I like your house, Freya. It's really cool."

"Well, thanks. I find it kind of lame sometimes but that's because it's my house. Other times, it's my favourite place ever. Hey Gab, you look a bit pale. Do you want a drink or something?"

"No, I'm fine thanks," replied Gab. For a few moments, Gab had forgotten about her stupidly complicated life scenario. Remembrance was all the more painful when it hit. Freya gave her a sympathetic look and got to work pumping up the lilo.

CHAPTER 42

July, mid-semester break

Gab and Freya stayed at Freya's place for three nights and by the end of the time, Gab had laughed more than any time she could remember. Freya's sisters Priya, Indira and Lena were funny, precocious, sweet. They accepted Gab into the fold naturally, just as they would have with any of their friends, treating her as if she were part of the family. For her part, Gab was eager to help out and fit in, assisting with chores and cleaning up. She joined in with family games and movies and this strange ecosystem of relationships was foreign and delightful. That secret, painful yearning she felt while watching Mr. C. with his children resurfaced, but was tempered by the joy of inclusion. By the end of the stay, she allowed herself to feel like one of the family. She had even talked with Priya and Freya together about the pregnancy. Both girls were encouraging and supportive of whatever decision Gab made. And being with Freya's family reminded her of those thoughts from her long walk that day she'd taken the pregnancy tests; of what it might mean to start her *own* family, with her own child, with the space and freedom to shape a life all of their own.

* * *

Gab wanted to make up her mind. Buoyed by the stay at Freya's home, she decided to phone Mr. C. and tell him. Being pregnant wasn't so bad, was it? It wasn't such a big deal—not the way Priya and Freya had talked about it. These things happened. It wasn't like a hundred years ago when Gab would have become a social pariah, forced into dingy backwaters or onto the streets; or like fifty years ago when she'd have been whisked away for the pregnancy, only to have her baby taken off her for being an 'unwed mother'. She hadn't ruined everything, had she?

Before the confidence of Priya and Freya could wear off, Gab decided phoned her old teacher.

"Hi, James speaking," he answered that chilly July evening.

"Mr. C? It's Gab. Gab Lander."

"Gab? How are you? How's uni? Great to hear from you!"

"Oh, thanks Mr. C. Yeah, um, uni's good. Really good," she said, trying to muster up some enthusiasm. It *had* been good, but she had not been feeling good.

"Have you settled into city life?"

"Yeah, it's okay. Lots of great food. My housemates are nice."

"I'm glad to hear it. What else is news?"

Gab was quiet; James could sense something was up. She didn't have the courage to launch in; where would she begin? How about, *I've been having nightmares? I feel so mixed up? I spent the night with a guy I don't know ... but I have no idea what actually happened? Except I've been horribly sick ... and it turns out I'm pregnant?* It all sounded so incredibly stupid inside her head.

Mr. C. didn't fill up the dead space with chatter; he was quiet.

"Mr. C? You still there?" Gab almost chickened out and hung up.

"Yeah, I'm still here. You still there, Gab?"

She smiled at his silly question. "Yeah, I'm here. You're not saying anything."

"Neither are you."

"It's just ... " she began timidly. She hated the thought that he would think less of her. But she had to tell him. It felt dishonest otherwise. He had to know the truth.

"I've been doing stupid stuff, Mr. C," she said finally.

"Oh ... you mean the typical uni stupid-stuff? Well ... that's okay, Gab. I mean, it's okay if you're okay. Are you okay?"

"I don't know ... it's just ... my mum's driving me crazy, Mr. C. She's calling *all* the time, texting me, making me feel guilty for coming here. She can't cope without me, and I feel bad for deserting her. I'm angry at her too, Mr. C, but she doesn't deserve it."

James was quiet for a moment.

"You haven't deserted her, Gab," he said quietly. "You haven't done anything that you need to feel guilty for."

"But I have!" Gab insisted. "She's at home on her own, and I'm out here living my life and ... " She trailed off. *And you have no idea what I have to say next*, she thought.

"Uni is exactly where you need to be, Gab. Isn't it?" spoke Mr. C. He was willing to reiterate this until it soaked in. Gab was silent, breathing hard.

"You have not done one thing," James continued, "not *one thing* that you need to feel guilty for, Gab. Really." He sounded so certain, so utterly convinced.

"Mr. C ... I've been sick over the semester ... "

"Have you?" he sounded concerned. "Have you been to the doctor?"

"Yes ... and ... don't worry, it's nothing major," Gab said automatically, not wanting to cause worry. "It's just ... it was a certain *kind* of sick, Mr. C ... " She trailed off. She breathed deeply. Then she shut her eyes tight and blocked out the world.

"Morning sickness."

There. She'd said it. She desperately hoped she wouldn't need to explain any more. She just couldn't.

James paused, only briefly. Had he picked up what Gab had put down?

"Okay," he said neutrally, slowly—as though considering his response. "Should I say congratulations, Gab? Or ... or is that not what you need to hear right now?"

"Mr. C ... " said Gab. She was so relieved he'd understood. And then something dawned on her. "That's the first time someone's said congratulations to me!"

"So ... it's okay then?" he asked gently. "Because if it doesn't fit with how you're feeling, that's okay ... I can say something else."

"No, it's fine," said Gab. "It really is." And she meant it.

"Well, good," said James, feeling more at ease. "Congratulations, Gab."

"Thanks Mr. C," continued Gab, "But, don't you think ... I mean ... I've really stuff up. I've wrecked everything! I'm so sorry." Her voice cracked.

"Wrecked what, Gab?" he asked. "You haven't wrecked anything, Gab."

"Yes, I have. You were so happy for me to come to uni. And now ... this."

"It's alright, Gab. It's your life, not mine. Life happens. And things often don't turn out as we'd planned."

"But what do I do next? I don't know what to do."

"You'll find a way through, Gab." Mr. C. was gently firm.

"But I won't!"

"You will, Gab. You will. Wherever this goes, it will be okay," said James.

That was a load off Gab's mind. Afterwards, Gab realised with surprise that no one—neither Freya, Priya, Saanvi nor even Mr.

C.—had acted like this was the end of the world, even though it felt like it to her. So maybe it wasn't. As long as she didn't think about what Gina's reaction might be, everything would be okay. She had no idea how or when she was going to tell her mother. She didn't want Gina weighing in on any decisions about her future.

CHAPTER 43

July, mid-semester break

The week after Gab told Mr. C, he and Melinda invited her to come and stay at their place for a weekend during her mid-semester break. They had a self-contained area upstairs, they said, which she was welcome to use. Gab was keen to see Mr. C, even if she was tentative about being back in her hometown. She didn't want any awkward conversations. She didn't want anyone to ask how she was, or how uni was going, and she didn't want to see her mother or even Tony. It was very unlikely she'd bump into Gina of course, but if she saw Tony, what would she say? He'd want to know why she had come back without telling anyone. She feared Tony's judgement; besides, she hadn't decided what to do yet.

On a Saturday morning in the last week of July, Gab packed her backpack and walked from the student apartment building, to the station where the regional bus would pick up its passengers. The three-hour trip reignited faint nausea and Gab closed her eyes and tried to doze.

And then, just like that, she was back in Wattle Gully Arriving in her hometown was like slipping back into an old version of herself, and Gab wasn't sure that she liked it, even if there was a certain comfort in familiarity.

The bus stopped outside the local post-office and Gab stepped off. Ten minutes and she'd be at the Cheng's. Three kilometres beyond that, her mother was probably sitting in her sunroom on her throne, watching reruns of old TV shows that she'd seen a thousand times already. But Gab wasn't going home. At least, she didn't plan on it.

Hand unconsciously resting on the small abdominal bump she was now sporting, Gab walked along the main street of town. She hoped to goodness she wouldn't run into anyone from work. She didn't, and she felt much safer once she was cutting through smaller streets towards Mr. and Mrs. C's place. James and Melinda. And Libby and Tyler, their kids. It would be so weird, she thought, but she wanted badly to see Mr. C. At the same time, she was scared.

After Gab arrived and settled in, she and the Chengs sat at the table for dinner. Then, James tucked Libby and Tyler into bed while Gab helped Melinda tidy up. It was fascinating for Gab to watch Mr. C. interact with his kids again; foreign and intriguing. With the kids settled, James, Melinda and Gab sat down again, sipping on tea and eating chocolates. Gab also watched the two of them interact. It was like listening to a piece of music, now with notes more discordant, now resolved into harmony; greater and lesser degrees of tension and resolution, two melodies dancing around each other in dynamic interaction.

"What are your plans once baby comes?" asked Melinda with a jarring mix of abruptness and warmth. Gab shrugged.

"I don't know," she said. "I'm not sure yet."

"When's baby due?"

"I'm seventeen weeks tomorrow. So, early January. Near my birthday," Gab said quietly.

"Gabrielle, babies are hard work," said Melinda knowingly. "I mean, it can be really tough. I can't imagine trying to do it all on my own." Gab nodded. She wasn't sure what else to say. "James and

I have talked about this," Melinda continued, "and we want you to know that you and baby are welcome to live here, if that's something you'd like."

This came entirely out of left field. Gab's thoughts stumbled over themselves. How did she feel about this? Too early to tell. Did they want an answer? Melinda sat looking at her, almost eagerly. Mr. C. just fiddled with the tag on his teabag.

"Oh wow, um okay, thanks," she said obligingly.

"What do you think?" Melinda pressed. "This weekend can be a test-run. We've had the upstairs sitting there empty since February, when Mum moved to the nursing home, so you'd have your own space. But we'd be here anytime you needed us." That seemed simultaneously nice and scary to Gab. It wasn't *bad* being there. It was just that Gab already felt like an intruder, imposing herself in a space where she really didn't belong.

Mr. C. changed the subject. "Tell me about more about uni, Gab. What was first semester like?"

"Oh yeah, it was really interesting," said Gab. "But hard to manage with … you know … feeling sick and stuff." Her words were cautious, but she gradually became animated as she told him more. "The subjects are great. There's so much I want to try out on my own land some day. I just wish I'd had more energy for study in the first semester, you know? I didn't really do very well in my exams." She faltered, because this was something of a sticking point for her.

Mr. C. nodded and smiled. "Sounds like you've been quite unwell the last few months. But I knew you'd enjoy uni, and you'll consolidate," he said. "One thing I noticed throughout school was that you quite enjoyed a challenge." Gab liked to think that he perceived her that way. So she looked down, embarrassed.

"Which brings us back to the baby," said Melinda. "Have you had much experience with babies, Gab?"

Gab felt a little interrogated, but she assumed the question was well meant; she didn't know how to avoid answering though, even if she wanted to.

"I looked after Jack," she said, and suddenly a streak of defensiveness arose. "He was born when I was eleven. And I've raised lots of baby animals." She felt like she needed to vouch for herself, defend her capacity. Mr. C. was staring off into the distance, as though trying to distance himself from his wife's question, but when he heard Gab's response, he was present again.

"You're an amazing big sister, Gab. You've done so much for Jack, and you'll well and truly manage this next season of life. Well," he slapped his knees, "It's time for some dessert, I reckon!" And with that, he was off to the freezer to get ice-creams for them all.

CHAPTER 44

"Gabrielle," said Melinda the next day, as Gab helped her hang out the washing. "Are you involved with your baby's father? Is he supporting you?"

Sure, Gab had known Mr. C. for years and years, and in a small town, where everyone rubbed shoulders with everyone else, she had noticed when Mr. C's wife showed up and moved in. But still—she wouldn't say she really *knew* Melinda. Melinda was being so kind, so warm and friendly in manner, but was oblivious to any possible sensation of discomfort which might result from her assumed right to *know*. Gab wouldn't have minded if Mr. C. had asked—but he wouldn't have, not like that. And that was exactly why she would have told him. But, Gab couldn't allow herself to be rude and ignore Melinda's question. She couldn't *not* reply, could she?

"Nah," she just said simply. Melinda pursed her lips.

"I can't stand it when that happens!" she said. "So often it's us women who are left to shoulder the blame and responsibility." Gab wasn't sure what she was being blamed for. She would have tended to agree with Melinda a few months ago, but things seemed different from here—from her own particular position.

"It's okay," Gab responded. "It's kind of easier this way." This logic did not at all fit with Melinda's framework of how things should be, but she simply pursed her lips tighter and kept on hanging the washing. Somehow, Gab sensed that if she mentioned how she was really feeling—her uncertainty as to whether to keep the baby in the first place—Melinda's sensibilities would be significantly more offended than they already were.

* * *

Upstairs at the Cheng's was comfortable, clean and airy. Gab quite liked it. She tried to imagine how things would be if she lived there—her and her baby. She did feel a slight inkling that Melinda was trying to rescue her though. The sense in that of being patronised, as though she *needed* rescuing, got to her a bit. It felt offensive to her dignity. *But then*, she told herself, *that wasn't quite fair*. Melinda was trying to do the right thing and the Chengs were being very generous, not just in their hospitality this long weekend, but in their offer of ongoing support. They had enough to juggle in their lives with two young kids, and they intended to charge Gab much less for rent and bills than she was paying in Melbourne. They weren't in it for the money. And it wasn't like having her around would make life easier for them.

So why were they doing it? Why was Melinda so eager to help? Gab didn't want to feel like she was being used in some weird, inexplicable way—but she couldn't help it. She couldn't explain it or demonstrate it or defend it. So she pushed the feeling aside, attributing it to her idiosyncratic and imbalanced sensitivities. That second night at the Chengs, she got into the clean double bed with paisley sheets and tried not to think about it. She listened to an audiobook about carbon-neutral pig farms instead.

CHAPTER 45

Monday morning. Rainy day. Gab peeped out to see grey sheets of water hitting the windowpane and promptly hid back under the covers. Seconds later, there was a knock on the bedroom door.

"Gabbyyyyyy. Gaaaabby?" It was Libby and Tyler. Aged four and six, Gab found them pretty cute. But this wasn't what Gab needed right now. Mind you, when she opened the door and they bounded onto the bed and wanted to snuggle with her and tell stories, she felt rather appeased. Still tired, though.

The kids hung out with her for several hours, Gab's patience ebbing and flowing, now less, now more. She wondered how she would cope with her own tiny person, all the time. Jack had been one thing—at least she'd still been able to go to school, mostly. She wondered about uni as she built block towers with Libby and Tyler. She really wanted to keep studying, to learn and expand her horizons. She wanted to work and do some good in the world. Was it even possible? Gab felt hopelessly defeated at the thought of giving it up so soon ... she had finally got there, found a home, started the course she wanted and figured out how to get around. Plus, Jack was okay and for the first time ever, she had physical space from her mum. And now, it was all crashing down around her only a few months in, and all because of one stupid night when she'd let her hair down for a few hours. A few hours!! She fought the sudden urge to smash the block tower she'd been building, and it scared her. She wasn't capable of being a mother! She'd felt annoyed when Libby and Tyler had come in that morning, and bored with their games at times. And now she wanted to smash their stupid block towers!

"Are you having a baby, Gabby?" Libby asked all of a sudden, pulling Gab out of her mental vortex. "Mummy told me not to ask you."

"Oh, um, yeah ... maybe," said Gab.

"What do you mean, *maybe*?" asked Libby. Gab grimaced; she'd stuck her foot in it.

"Is it in your tummy or not?" Libby continued, with more than a hint of her mother's directness.

"Yeah," said Gab.

"Is it a boy or girl?" asked Libby. "I hope it's a girl! You could call it Posie. Or Benita. I have a doll called Benita."

"I want it to be a boy!" frowned Tyler. "And his name should be Tyler."

Gab smirked.

"It's a surprise," she told the kids.

"But how will you know what clothes to buy?" asked Libby. "Blue or pink?"

"Oh, that doesn't matter," said Gab. "Girls can wear blue and boys can wear pink, if they want."

"No, they can't!" argued Tyler.

"Well, they can actually!" said Libby, deciding suddenly to side with Gab. Her additional two years of age were helpful in grasping this. "And they can wear yellow and white and red and purple. Even rainbow!"

"You forgot green!" said Tyler. "That's *my* favourite colour."

At that moment, Mr. C. knocked on the door.

"Sorry Gab," he said, "I hope the kids haven't been bothering you too much."

"Dadddddyyyy, we never *bother*!" chided Libby. Mr. C. raised his eyebrows and winked at Gab.

"Nah, it's fine Mr. C. It's all good."

"I saw you do winky-eye, Daddy! What did it mean?" demanded Libby. Nothing got past her!

"Time for a walk to the park, you munchkins," said Mr. C. swinging a child up onto each side of his waist. They went off singing 'The Ants Go Marching' and Gab was left sitting amongst a land of block towers, animals and weird square-shaped block-people.

A few moments later, Melinda knocked at the door.

"Can I come in?" she asked.

"Yep," said Gab. "Come in." Melinda sat down at the small, round kitchen table. Gab got up off the floor and joined her there.

"I've been thinking about you," said Melinda to Gab.

"Oh," said Gab. "Good things or bad things?" She wondered if Melinda had suddenly changed her mind about the rental offer. She felt hope and disappointment at once.

"Oh, nothing like that," smiled Melinda, though a little tersely. "I've been thinking about the father of your baby." Gab stiffened. Melinda's directness was still jarring.

"It's okay, Mel, really," said Gab, trying to diffuse tension and redirect the conversation.

"The thing is, honey," said Mel, "it's not okay. That little baby has the right to know its father. He or she will ask about their daddy. They'll notice very quickly that other kids have a dad and that they don't."

Internally, Gab bristled. *So what?!* she wanted to say. But she didn't. There was no point biting the hand that was feeding her—tonight's meal, anyhow. So, she was quiet and unknowingly frowned a little.

"Kids always do better with both parents," continued Melinda. "They have a right to both parents. It's just how things are." Melinda got up. "Anyhow, I'll give you some space to think about it. You know my thoughts on the topic." Gab was silent. Melinda turned as she reached the door. "You know it's not a criticism, Gab. I'm just trying to help, okay?" She smiled. Gab sat still, unmoving. A little unnerved, Melinda turned back towards the door.

Just as she pulled it open, Gab stood up, compelled, pushed, and said, "I grew up without a dad, Melinda."

CHAPTER 46

Melinda recovered from this quickly and promptly converted it into her own ammunition.

"So, you know what it feels like, Gab. All the more reason to give this some serious thought."

"But Melinda," said Gab, "I'm okay. I didn't have a dad and I'm fine."

"Of course you are, honey," Melinda answered.

"But aren't you saying that I'm somehow deficient? Because I didn't grow up with a dad?" Gab struggled to keep her voice polite. She didn't want to be rude. Melinda had invited her into her home, into her very family. More powerful than these superego admonitions, however, was the thought of hurting Mr. C. by being rude to his wife.

"No, not at all honey," crooned Melinda, coming back towards her again. "I'm talking about best case scenarios here, and what we can do to make sure your little baby has the best shot at life."

"It's just a little bit complicated, Mel," said Gab.

"I'm sure it is," agreed Melinda, "but the truth is always best. The truth will set you free."

Gab sighed, sat down again and laid her head on the table. She felt angry, so angry—at herself.

"I ... screwed ... up," she said quietly. "I screwed up so bad!!" She said it loudly the second time, banging the table with her fist. Then she looked up. "I'm SO STUPID! So so so STUPID!" She grabbed the sides of her head in frustration. She wanted to pummel herself, to pull all her hair out! But Melinda was watching and what if she thought Gab was crazy and called the hospital or the police? More mental whiplash at those ideas; Gab stood up quickly again, knocking over her chair and slapping her hands on the table. She'd never lost it like this before.

"We all make mistakes, Gab," Melinda said, her voice quaking slightly in shock at Gab's outburst. "We all make mistakes. And you made a mistake."

This was inadvertently the perfect thing for Melinda to say to Gab at that moment—but not in the way Melinda intended. Because now, instead of beating *herself* up about it all, Gab was suddenly ready to *fight* for herself. She had been incited—incited into recognising the person she was, into standing up tall. What she had done at that party was not a mistake. It *was* a mistake, and it *wasn't* a mistake. Life wasn't as simple as black and white. She had to make the best of how things were. And something came into focus right in that moment; Gab knew her own mind. She took a breath. This sense of clarity had re-grounded her. The rollercoaster had pulled in.

She looked Mel right in the eye and took a deep breath.

"I'm not involving this baby's father," she said. She didn't add that it would hurt too many people to do so and would make her look like a cheating wench. "He doesn't know about the baby." She hadn't planned to tell Melinda all this, but now that she'd started, she would continue. "And I'm *not* going to tell him."

"But how could you do that to him? To your child?" Melinda was aghast.

"Mel, I know what it's like to grow up without a dad. And what I've always wanted to know is—did he leave because he didn't want me? Did he know my mum was pregnant? Did he go because of me? I'm not going to risk that for my child. I'm not going to risk having to tell my baby it was rejected before it was even born!" The thought of it made her want to vomit. "I'd rather tell my child that their father really just had no idea!"

"Won't your child blame you, then? asked Melinda. "Won't they want to know why you never told him? And … does this mean you aren't even in a relationship with the baby's father?" Melinda struggled to hide her disapproval. It was just so far from her own experience; she couldn't imagine it.

"It doesn't matter," said Gab. "And, um, thanks for your kind offer to let me live here once I have the baby. It's really nice of you. But … I'm going to stay at uni and keep studying."

She didn't talk about whether or not she would keep the baby. It seemed that Melinda assumed she would.

CHAPTER 47

Melinda sat with James in bed that night, near tears.

"It's just such a mess, James! She doesn't want to tell the father. She doesn't want to stay here. She doesn't know what she's doing!"

James' compassion for his wife mingled with his firm belief in Gab's capabilities. So, he put an arm around his wife and didn't say anything.

"James, say something!" she demanded. "We can't let this happen! We can't leave this poor girl to fend for herself!"

"Yes, support for Gab is vital," said James, latching onto the one point in his wife's comment that he could agree with unreservedly. "But perhaps that support could look a bit different to what we originally imagined. So she doesn't want to live here; that's entirely her right. It doesn't mean we stop being here for her, if and when she needs it."

"But James!" contested his wife, "I just *can't* see how this will work for her. That poor baby..."

"Mel," James turned to face his wife, "Gab is clever. She's a problem-solver. She makes things work. I have no doubt that she'll find a way forward. And maybe it's more important to support that tenacity than to hold onto what we might think is a good solution."

Melinda sighed. This was typical of James. He always seemed to dampen her passion and bring her visions down to earth with his pragmatism. Maybe she needed it, she reflected, even if it was frustratingly annoying.

"Have I been too full on?" asked Melinda, disappointed in herself. She wanted to help; she wanted badly to do the right thing.

James knew not to answer her question directly.

"You're fine, Mel. We're all figuring this out as we go along. Let's just give Gab some space. She'll spread her wings. I know she will."

CHAPTER 48

July

Gab was staring out the window on the bus ride back to Melbourne, mindless watching the scenery pass by: paddocks green from the winter rains, cows, horses, sheep ... the occasional wallaby. Troubled thoughts of her conversations with Melinda turned in her mind. A flutter in her abdomen drew her attention.

Was it ... ?

She laid her palm across on her abdomen. And she felt the gentlest, subtlest fluttery bump against her hand. There it was again! Her heart fluttered then too, and she couldn't suppress a grin; happy tears welled up in her eyes. She put both hands on her belly.

And she suddenly realised how badly she wanted to prove Melinda wrong. This was an opportunity ... an opportunity to start again, to start her own family and to prove that she could do it. This baby was the beginning of something different. With this baby, Gab wouldn't be Gina's daughter so much as she would be this child's mother. *She* would be the foundational locus of a new family; this baby would be her family. She wanted that so badly. She didn't know how to make it happen or how to be a good mother, or whether she could do it, but she wanted it so, so much. She wanted someone to whom she could give what she had never received from her own family, from her mother—space to be heard, encouragement, belief, companionship. She imagined being the person who believed in her child unreservedly. Could she?

She felt strongly then how meaningful life *could* be; how full of purpose. It wasn't a hollow drive, an empty structure of heavy responsibility that lay upon her without substance; it was whole. It was a purpose that began inside her very self and radiated outwards with strength and potent energy. She realised for a moment, in that moment, she had found herself. It was a tenuous grasp; it wasn't permanent or static. But it was real.

* * *

"Freya, I'm going to keep my baby!" It was the first thing Gab said as she entered Freya's room, back from her trip to Wattle Gully, back from James and Melinda's, back from the valley of indecision and haze. She had felt her baby's first kick on the bus ride back to the city, and that was that. She knew.

Freya rose up from her bed, her hands over her mouth in surprised delight.

"Really, Gab? Really? Congratulations!" She came over and hugged her friend. "I mean, I would have supported your decision either way, one hundred percent ... but a real live baby!! You're going to be amazing!"

Gab looked down. "Thanks. Do you think so?"

"I know it! How did you decide?"

Gab grinned.

"Felt its first kick on the way home!"

"Ohhhh!" Freya whispered and hugged her again.

"It made it so real, Freya," said Gab. "It's not just an idea any-more. It's real." In that moment, Gab felt warm, whole, decisive.

"And besides," she added, a little sheepishly, "I want to prove to Melinda wrong." Gab went and sat on Freya's bed.

"Melinda is Mr. C's wife, right?" said Freya, plopping into her blue and purple furry beanbag. "Why? What did she do?"

"She just doesn't like the whole situation," said Gab. "She was trying to fix it, I think. She's convinced my baby needs a father in its life. And she was telling me how hard and exhausting parenting is, so I shouldn't try to do it on my own. I didn't tell her I hadn't even decided on keeping the baby yet." Gab unconsciously had her hand on her slightly protruding abdomen. "She would have fainted!"

"It's not for her to judge!" Freya exclaimed. "It's not her life! But what about Mr. C.? He's a good guy, right? What did he do while she was busy intruding?"

"Well, she mostly said those things when he wasn't around … "

"No!! The shrew! What else did she say?"

Gab laughed at Freya's vocal disapproval.

"She invited me to come live with them once the baby is born."

"Really? What did you say?" asked Freya, her dark eyebrows raised high.

"I said no."

"You did?"

"Yeah. It was just … I don't know. Coming from Melinda, it made me feel … crowded in. Claustrophobic." Gab paused. "But, she didn't *mean* to impose, Freya. She was only trying to help. So I feel really bad for getting mad at her, and for saying no to the invitation," confessed Gab.

"It's okay to feel mad when someone who hardly knows you thinks they have a right to make decisions for you!" maintained Freya, with characteristic insight. "And moving in there is a big decision. You have to do what's best for you, not what *Melinda* thinks is best for you."

Gab was quiet for a minute and began chewing on her nails distractedly.

"Are you okay?" Freya asked.

"Yeah, I'm okay." Gab regained her focus. "It wasn't all bad. It kind of felt like a holiday most of the time and Mr. C. was great. And, oh my gosh, Freya," Gab smiled at her memories of Libby and Tyler, "their kids are hilarious! If my kid is that funny, I'll be laughing all the time."

"What did they do?"

"Oh, I dunno, just said funny, unfiltered stuff. Tyler, the four-year-old, he wants me to call the baby Tyler, after him. They must have heard me talking with their mum and dad about the baby, because they just asked me straight out and were so honest about it. They weren't embarrassed at all."

"Cute!"

"Yeah. And a little bit exhausting too. But that made me realise something else," Gab added.

"What's that?" asked Freya, wondering in awe what other epiphanies Gab might have had over that weekend.

"If I'm keeping the baby, I want to stay at uni too; I really do. It was only when I thought about moving back to Wattle Gully that I realised it ... It's taken so much to get here Freya, and I don't want to give it up."

"This is so good," said Freya. "You are so strong."

"I don't know if I can do it, though. Is it even possible?"

"You won't know until you try," reasoned Freya.

"I can't believe this baby is real, Freya," said Gab. "And it's mine."

CHAPTER 49

The break between first and second semesters was drawing to a close. Gab and Freya were sitting in the lounge-room of their apartment while Steph made herself a spinach and coconut-water smoothie. Gab hadn't discussed her plans for continuing uni with the other girls in her apartment yet, but they'd figured out she was pregnant. Steph was only half listening to Freya and Gab's conversation, but her ears pricked up when she realised they were discussing whether Gab would take the baby to lectures. Steph wheeled around.

"We are *not* having that baby here!" she interjected, cutting Gab off mid-sentence. "Why would you even *think* that might be okay? We'd never get any study done!" Gab pretended it didn't cut deeply to hear the rejection straight out.

"I never said I was staying here," said Gab quietly.

"Well, it sounds like you might be considering it!" retorted Steph. "So, you're keeping the baby?"

"Hang on, hold off!" said Freya. "Who said Gab couldn't stay here?"

"Well, will she be paying rent for two?"

"Steph!" Freya cried.

Gab got up and walked out the door and towards the elevator, Freya following behind. Gab knew it wouldn't be easy; she wasn't going to inflict the new circumstances on the others without their consent. She just hadn't expected to be so flatly shunned, as if she had done something wrong by choosing to keep her baby. It wasn't the baby's fault that it would cry; they'd all started off that way. And it wasn't the baby's choice to come into the world. Was Steph trying to punish her? Gab was upset and angry. Didn't Steph understand that she couldn't just go home to her mum or dad like *she* could? Didn't Steph realise that this wasn't what Gab had *wanted*? Gab hated Steph's assumptions, Steph's affluence and Steph's options.

Freya followed Gab into the elevator and they rode down in silence. But as soon as they stepped outside and onto the lawn, Freya said, "Don't listen to her, Gab. She has no right to talk to you like that."

"She doesn't understand!" cried Gab, throwing her arms up in the air. "It could have been any of us!"

"I know."

"I wouldn't treat her that way if *she* was having a baby! I'd want to support her and help her out. I'd think it was great if she wanted to keep going with uni, instead of treating her like a criminal who was somehow doing something wrong!" Gab's voice cracked with pent-up emotion.

"Yeah, I know."

"I mean, I get it! She doesn't want a baby waking her up at all hours of the night. And yeah, maybe a baby doesn't really fit into uni life. But does she have to be so mean about it?" Gab blinked back tears.

"No, she doesn't," said Freya earnestly, sitting down on a bench.

"What am I going to do, Freya?"

"Let's go grab some dumplings, Gab. Come on." Freya took her friend's arm. Gab was too preoccupied to argue. She and Freya walked towards Dumpling King. Arriving, they sat down at a table in the little dumpling house and Freya grabbed a napkin and then borrowed a pen from one of the waiters.

"Let's work out your options, Gab," she said. "Let's brainstorm."

"Okay," Gab agreed. "But let's order food first!" Now that her morning sickness had mostly abated, she was hungry all the time. Dumplings and drinks were ordered and the young women threw around ideas for Gab's future living arrangements. They came up with a list of options:

Move back to Mum's (uni break or quit or transfer)
Move to Chengs' (uni break or quit or transfer)
Stay at current apartment??
Rent somewhere near uni— apartment, share house, room for rent?

"Will you need a break from uni at the start?" asked Freya. "I mean, having a new baby is a big deal."

"I just ... I *really* want to continue," said Gab. "I feel like it gives me something to look forward to; something to work towards." Freya nodded. "And," Gab added, "it gives me a reason to stay in the city instead of going back to Mum's. I know she'll try and convince me, I *know* she will ... when I finally tell her. And I'm not good at saying no to her. Uni gives me that reason to say no."

"You're allowed to say no for your own sake, Gab," said Freya quietly, taking a sip of the bubble tea that had just been delivered to their table.

"I know. But I'll feel more comfortable with a reason."

Freya nodded. "Have you thought about studying part-time?"

"Yeah, I've been wondering about it. I reckon it would be ideal. But ... then I'll stop receiving Youth Allowance, won't I? You have to be studying full time." Gab's face fell. "There's be no way I'll be able to afford it."

Freya scrunched up her face to think until her face lit up again. "But you'll get a parenting allowance instead or something, won't you?"

"Maybe?"

"Well, we can cross your mum and the Chengs off the housing list since you want to stay here at uni," said Freya, doing just that. "They weren't really options to begin with. It just made the list look better," she said.

"And cross off our current apartment," said Gab. "Steph won't have it. What am I going to do, Frey? How can I afford to go any-where by myself? I'm going to end up on the streets!"

"That is *not* going to happen, Gab," said Freya adamantly. "No way. My mum would have you at her place before you even came close to that. I know you want your own space," she added, "but at least Mum and Dad's is a manageable distance from uni."

Gab nodded. "But would they really let me?"

"No question," said Freya. "But don't give up too quickly. Single room student accommodation might not cost much more than what you're paying now." Freya's positivity was contagious because Gab was looking for signs of hope.

"Maybe I can stay in our same building and get a studio room!" Gab suggested. "That wouldn't be much hassle. Then we'd still be neighbours!" Freya nodded enthusiastically.

Just then, a smiling waitress brought out several baskets of steam-ing dim sims and pork-buns, placing them onto the girls' table. Filling up her plate, Gab looked at the mouth-watering, tender little bodies of deliciousness swimming in soy sauce. Soothed by the sense of possibilities now opening up, Gab tucked in with gusto, with Freya not far behind.

CHAPTER 50

The girls finished their meal and got up to pay. Back home, they hung out in Gab's room with their laptops, researching possibilities. The first thing Gab did was to contact the company who leased their current building as student accommodation.

Hi, how can I help you? began the online conversation, as a sales rep. reached out to Gab.

Hi, Gab wrote. *I'm a student currently living in your Parkville building in a four-bedroom apartment. Next year I need a one-bedroom studio instead because I'm having a baby, but I'd like to stay in the same building. Do you accept applications from people with an infant?*

Long pause.

No, I'm sorry. Our policy doesn't allow applications from students with infants. Is there anything else I can help you with?

No thanks, that's all.

Enjoy your day.

Bye.

She'd ended the conversation too quickly, out of politeness, but moments later she wished she'd pushed harder. Then she tried another company nearby. And another. And the answer was the same. *No infants.* It seemed so unfair.

"I just don't get it!" exclaimed Gab. "It's like they're punishing you for having a baby! For being a parent! How can they discriminate like that? Don't they think parents can be students too?"

"Gab," said Freya with resolve in her voice, and Gab looked up. "Why don't you and I rent an apartment together? Not student blocks … just, you know, a private rental?"

There was a pleasant whooshing sensation somewhere in the region of Gab's stomach. "Freya … really?" Her eyes welled up. "Are you sure? You don't have to say that to be nice. Steph's right. Being around me and my baby will be so disruptive. You'll regret it and then I'll feel awful."

"I won't regret it, Gab," said Freya firmly. "I'd love it! Let's check out two-bedroom apartments; forget student accommodation. I've lived with babies before … I remember when my little sisters were born. And loads of my cousins have kids. It's not anything strange or different to what I'm used to."

"But Freya, you can't!" insisted Gab, desperately wanting to take up the offer but feeling she couldn't possibly inconvenience Freya in this way. It wasn't worth it for her friend. "Besides," she added, "it's probably way more expensive to rent properly than to get student accommodation."

"Well, let's take a look first. There's no harm in doing that. Unless you really do prefer to be on your own. I totally respect that if you prefer it."

Gab was silent for a moment, thinking. She couldn't disrupt her friend's life like this. But then again, Freya had offered … and Gab was on the verge of desperation. As Gab thought about it, it dawned on her that maybe she should—she could—take Freya's kind gesture at face value; trust it.

"Freya … I'd love to share—only, as long as it's not a burden for you."

"Let's go for it, Gab."

It was settled. Gab couldn't argue with Freya anymore, and didn't want to. And, to her surprise, the two-bedroom rentals they looked up nearby were cheaper than their current accommodation.

"It'll be harder to get a place," said Freya realistically. "And we'll have to pay utility bills, which we don't have to do here. *And* we'll need furniture. But," she continued, "we've got a rental history here. Let's just apply for everything we can and see what happens! Furniture we can worry about later."

* * *

The two girls spent the first four weekends of semester two trekking around to open house inspections. They weren't fussy in what they were looking for, as long as the apartment bedrooms didn't share a wall, which would minimise the transfer of night-noise. Freya assured Gab that she was a deep sleeper who hardly woke to anything.

By week five, they had applied for more than twenty apartments. When they received the phone call telling them they'd finally been successful, they were delighted. In their elation, they immediately began planning the furnishing of their apartment—simple, inexpensive, baby-friendly. They would move in in November.

It was time to tell Steph and Morgan.

"Ohhhhh," said Steph, when they broke the news. "I was looking forward to having a baby around here!" Gab and Freya looked at each other incredulously. But it didn't matter. They had a way forward, and it was a good one. Gab could focus on making the most of her semester two studies, notwithstanding a gradually swelling abdomen.

September, 22 weeks pregnant

"Hey Brian, how are you? May I please speak with Jack?"

Gab, Freya and Morgan were at the Royal Botanic Gardens this morning. It was early spring; flowering bulbs were beginning to bloom and trees were clothed in fresh, vibrant spring greens. Freya and Morgan were lying on the grass, Morgan reading, Freya sketching; Gab wandered a little way off and took the opportunity to call her brother.

Brian handed the phone to Jack.

"Hey Jack!" said Gab. "How are you, matey?"

"Hi Gabby! I'm good," said Jack. Gab loved hearing his voice.

"What have you been up to?" asked Gab.

"Dad's taking me to the waterpark on the weekend!" exclaimed Jack, perking up. "I'm going to wear my new board shorts. And we're gonna go on the giant waterslide and have ice cream!"

"Wow, Jack, that sounds amazing!" said Gab.

"I know!" said Jack, "I've never been to the waterpark before."

"So you're enjoying living with your dad then?" asked Gab.

"Yeah!" Jack answered with enthusiasm.

"How's school?"

"Bo-ring." Jack's enthusiasm instantly evaporated.

"Doing your readers?"

"Not *every* night," he admitted. "But most nights, Gab!"

"Did you do one last night?" she asked.

"Yep," Jack replied. "I read a book about a duck named Quacky-Lacky."

"Good book?"

"Nah, it was boring!" said Jack. *Boring*—there was that favourite word again.

"Oh. Well, at least you had a go at reading it," Gab encouraged.

"My reading's getting pretty good now, Gab. I can read long words."

"I'm so glad to hear it! What's the longest word you can read?" she asked.

"Probably like, *dinosaur*. And I can spell 'there' in three different ways!"

"That's great, Jack! Dinosaur is a giant word and the *theirs* are super tricky!"

"Do you have to do readers at your grown-up school?" asked Jack.

"Yeah I do. I have to go to class, just like at school, and then do lots of homework."

"Sounds bo-ring."

Gab laughed. "Nah, it's great actually." Jack was too stunned by the thought Gab was enjoying her 'readers' to say anything more on that topic.

"Have you spoken to Mum lately, Jack?"

"Oh, yeah," he said, and she could hear the rolling eyes in his tone. "Bo-ring!"

"Does she call you?" Gab was curious.

"Sometimes. Mostly on Sundays. I don't want to talk to her, cos it's boring, but Dad says I have to," Jack replied.

"What does she say to you?"

"Mostly the usual stuff. Like, *How are you going? Are you doing your homework?*. Pretty much the same as you."

"Am I boring to talk to?" asked Gab. The comparison stung.

"Nah, cos you're fun."

"Why's Mum boring then?"

"Oh, she just grumps at me and says, *Why don't you come back and visit me?*" Jack mimicked Gina's whiney-voice.

"And you don't want to?"

"No. Cos *you're* not there!" Jack explained. Gab wasn't sure if that made her feel better or worse.

"Hey Jack," said Gab, feeling like she was stepping off the edge of a precipice. "I gotta tell you something really important."

"Like a secret?"

"Yeah, exactly. A secret."

"I'm the best secret knower!" said Jack. "What is it? Spill the guts, Gab."

"Ha. Well, this one's a really, *really* big secret, okay Jack?" she said tentatively.

"Yeah! Tell me!"

"I'm … ummm … it's a bit hard to say."

"Why? Is it a tongue-twister? I can do tongue-twisters! Look, I can say Peter-Piper-Pecka-Pippa … oh, I forgot." Gab laughed despite herself, and then launched in. There was nothing else for it.

"Jack … you know how sometimes ladies have babies in their tummies?"

"Yeah, like Mrs. Taylor," said Jack knowingly.

"Who's that?" asked Gab.

"My art teacher at my school." Jack had started that year at a primary school nearer to Brian's.

"Is she pregnant?"

"Yeah! Her tummy's bigger 'an a basketball! And her legs are like sticks!"

"Oh dear! Poor Mrs. Taylor. But yeah Jack, just like that. Pregnant like Mrs. Taylor. Well, guess what?"

"What?" asked Jack. Gab's heart began pounding.

"I have a baby now too!" There. She'd done it. She exhaled.

"Where?!" asked Jack, incredulous.

"In my tummy, just like Mrs. Taylor," explained Gab.

"WHAAAAT???" exclaimed Jack. "But Gab! Where'd you get it?"

"Oh ... um, I'll tell you that some other time," Gab replied awkwardly.

"Was it magic?"

"Well, um ... no ... in a way ... Anyhow, the thing is Jack, this baby is a really big, giant secret." Gab grimaced.

"Oh yeah, I know *that*. But when can I see the baby, Gabby? Can I hold it?"

"Not yet, Jack. In a couple of months."

"Ohhhh, why?"

"It has to grow big enough first. It's too little now and it's still in my tummy. And guess what Jack? You'll be its uncle!"

"WHAT???" Jack was incredulous again. "But I'm just a kid!"

"Kids can be uncles. You'll be Uncle Jack!"

"Well, that's just *weird*!" said Jack. "My friends won't even believe me."

"Remember Jack, it's a secret." Gab really questioned whether she'd done the right thing in telling Jack. But then, how could she not? It was Jack. She wanted to share it with him.

"But when can I tell? Can I tell Dad?"

"Yeah, you can tell your dad. Just him, okay? But the main person I don't want you to tell is Mum."

"Oh yeahhhh, I know *that*," said Jack, as if it was the most obvious thing in the world. "Cos Mum will get all ... you know ... like, freaking out and stuff."

"Yeah, I think she will."

"But I think a baby's cool!"

"Thanks Jack! That means a lot to me."

"You're welcome."

"Can I talk with your dad now?"

"Okay, bye!"

"Bye, Jack."

Now that Gab had told Jack, it was easier to tell Brian. She didn't go into much detail with Brian; she didn't need to. She just explained that she was twenty-two weeks pregnant, that she was going to continue at uni once she had the baby, and that her mum didn't know yet.

"Brian, I've asked Jack not to tell Mum yet," she said. "I really don't want her freaking out about it."

"Yeah, yeah, I know what you mean, Gab. I won't say a word." Brian wondered when Gab *was* planning to tell Gina.

"Thanks," replied Gab. "Could you please remind Jack to keep it a secret too?"

"Sure, sure," agreed Brian. "You alright, Gabby?"

"I guess," answered Gab, not even sure of the answer.

"Unexpected?"

"Yeah."

"That's okay," said Brian, "Life's like that sometimes, isn't it? Unexpected."

"Yeah, it is," agreed Gab, grateful for Brian's nonchalance.

"You take care then, Gab. Yell out if you need anything," he said to her.

"Thanks Brian, I really appreciate it," said Gab.

"No worries, love. Hooroo."

"See ya, Brian," said Gab. And that was that.

CHAPTER 52

September, 24 weeks pregnant

Gab was looking for her keys in a flowerbed when her phone rang. She'd been sitting on a retaining wall eating a pulled pork wrap and thoroughly enjoying it when the keys had fallen from her lap. Face half buried in a sea of flowering dahlias, she found her keys and stood up, then pulled her phone from her pocket.

The vibrating screen read: MUM, and Gab's appetite drained away. *Damn*, she thought. Guilt compelled her to answer however, because she'd already ignored the seven phone calls in the last three days, and it was really getting ridiculous now.

"Hi Gina," said Gab.

"Gabrielle, Gabrielle, Gabrielle," her mother was sobbing. "What have you done? *What have you done*?!" Gab cleared her throat, grabbed the remains of her wrap and looked for a secluded spot between buildings.

"What is it, Mum?" she asked quietly, her stomach having dropped to the ground, half-digested lunch and all.

"Oh Gabrielle, Gabrielle! How could you! I warned you!"

"MUM! *What* did you warn me about?"

"About the dangers of university, Gabrielle! The dangers! You ignored my warnings, and now *this* ... THIS!"

"MUM! Please, *what* has happened?" Gab knew exactly what, but she sure as heck wasn't going to say it.

"This ... this ... this DISASTER! This SIN! This PREGNANCY" squawked her mother.

"Oh," said Gab, "you mean the one where I have a baby, just like you did with Jack and me?" Boom. She'd smacked that one out of the park, and she knew it. But the satisfaction was short lived, because it only made Gina wail louder.

"What will you *do,* Gabrielle? What will you DO? You can't look after a baby! Oh, I can't believe this has happened to me!"

"Happened to *you*, Mum? What the hell do you mean? Nothing's happened to *you*, actually. What about *me*?"

"Oh, I think we know what's happened to *you*!" Gab's mother snorted. "We know perfectly well." The only thing that stopped Gab from emitting an unhinged roar was the fact that there were plenty of other people nearby. She hung up instead, and stormed off towards nowhere, anywhere, she didn't know where.

Her phone rang again.

MUM.

"Damn you!" cried Gab. But she was so mad that she wanted it to keep going. She was storing up retorts instant by instant, darts to send hurtling towards her mother one after the other after the other. She wanted a chance to throw them.

"WHAT is it, Mum? I don't think you could improve on your own hypocrisy. It's outstanding," Gab said acerbically.

"Gabrielle," her mother had flipped into her slow breathing, pseudo-guru mode. "I don't want to fight. Let's talk like rational adults."

"O-kay" said Gab, with clenched teeth, not missing the irony in her mother's words. "Go then."

"What are you going to do?" demanded Gina.

"Why do you want to know?" Gab retorted.

"I'm your mother. It's my right to know."

"Being my mother doesn't give you a *right* to know!"

"Blood is thicker than water," said Gina, with that infuriating calmness.

"And milkshakes are thicker than orange juice! So what!" Gab rejoindered.

"*Gabrielle.*"

"How *dare* you tell me not to fight, Mum. YOU were the one who phoned *me* in hysterics!"

"Are you calling me *hysterical*? Are you *blaming me* for this situation? Are you saying *I* have problems?"

"Yeah, the ones you've regaled me with night and day my entire life! Mum, this is going nowhere. Yes, I'm pregnant. I didn't plan it. It's just how things are." Gab burst into tears. "How did you find out?"

"*Jack* told me." She was emphatic and breathy.

Gab couldn't blame Jack, of course. She knew she'd been taking a risk in telling him, but she'd wanted him to know. Maybe she was even a little bit pleased that she'd been relieved of the task herself— of finding the right moment and the right way, which didn't exist anyhow.

Then Gab took matters into her own hands. She took a breath and held her nerve. She didn't vent anymore in reactive, entirely reasonable anger; but she contained the force of that anger within the bounds of herself, and that gave her whole being a greater presence, her words a greater weight in themselves, perhaps more than any screaming match could have done.

"Mum, I'm pregnant and it's okay. I'm organising stuff and working it all out. I'm going to be fine and I don't need anything from you. I'll let you know when the baby arrives. Take care, Mum. Bye."

And with that, she hung up and sat down again on a nearby bench. She stared at the last of her pulled-pork wrap. If she hadn't been growing another human being inside her, she would have thrown it into the bin in residual disgust. As it was, she was still hungry and she certainly wasn't going to let Gina take those last delicious mouthfuls away from her, on top of everything else she'd done. She shoved the last three mouthfuls in with a vengeance.

But it wasn't over, because just as she stood up, Gina texted.

Just tell me it wasn't an Asian boy. Or an Indian. They're everywhere in the city!

Gab recoiled. She thought of Saanvi's kindness and bristled with rage. She thought of Mr Cheng and shook her head at her mother's absolute wilful ignorance.

You are so racist, Mum! Get a life! she texted back. She made a mental note to marry 'an Indian' or 'an Asian' in future.

And then, she looked at her mother's number on her phone screen and tapped, 'BLOCK CONTACT'.

CHAPTER 53

October, November

Gab studied hard during second semester. That made her feel more like the old self she knew. Exams came, and she did much better in them than she had in first semester when she had been feeling horrendously sick and thoroughly exhausted every day. Plus, having blocked Gina's calls had cleared up an incredible amount of brain space and emotional energy for Gab. And she needed it.

Moving day was approaching quickly, and Gab and Freya were having a blast planning their new home. Gab had raised Jack on a shoestring when it came to baby equipment, so, unlike other soon-to-be mothers attending the hospital's childbirth education classes, she was quite happy to keep things simple. She found a second-hand cot, a used but excellent pram, and bags of quickly-outgrown baby clothes from a family who was happy to sell them to her for a minimal price. A baby carrier and a car seat were the only things she bought new—and the nappies of course. Her small bedroom was becoming a baby supplies warehouse and she had no idea how she was going to get everything to the new apartment.

She didn't want to ask Tony to help her move again. She had't spoken to him but assumed Gina had shared the pregnancy news; Gab felt embarrassed and didn't know what she would say to him even if they did talk. In reality, Tony would have done exactly what he did when Gina had fallen pregnant both times—been happy to help. But the more Gab put off talking to him, the scarier it seemed.

However, when Gab raised the question of moving logistics with Freya, Freya informed her with surprise that her dad and the younger girls were planning to come and help. It was almost assumed for Freya, though of course she'd asked as a matter of politeness—but it was just what their family did. Gab was happily folded into that, and it was a relief and a weight off her mind, because she didn't have to ask Tony or Brian, who had already given too much.

Moving day came in November, a week after both girls had finished exams. It was just the two of them left in the apartment now. Morgan had made a quick dash for home as soon as exams were finished—but not before profusely wishing Gab good luck and gifting her with a generous bag of baby goodies. Steph had gone on holidays to Queensland.

"All the best, Gab," Morgan had smiled, on the morning of her departure. "I hope it all goes really well in the new place."

"Yeah, with the *baby*," said Steph, arms crossed, with a little too much emphasis on the last word. It was awkward.

"Don't worry about her," said Freya later on. "You never have to see her again after this!"

It didn't really make Gab feel any better, but it was true. Another new season was just around the corner.

CHAPTER 54

Moving day arrived. Freya's dad, Anders, along with Indira and Lena, arrived bright and early—8:00AM. After Freya provided everyone with mugs of steaming, fragrant coffee, the five worked together in loading up the four-wheel-drive. Once packed, Anders and Freya ferried the load to the girls' new place and unpacked, while Gab, Indira and Lena stacked, cleaned and organised at the old quarters, ready to load up again once Freya and Anders returned with the vehicle.

The new apartment was on the first floor of a small block of flats. The girls' bedrooms were on opposite sides of the dwelling, which Gab desperately hoped would mitigate most of the baby-noise before it reached Freya. There was no nursery; Gab hadn't even thought of putting the baby in a separate room. When Freya had suggested it, both girls had baulked at the price difference be-tween two- and three-bedroom flats in Parkville. So a two-bedroom apartment it was.

There was no large furniture to transport across, so, despite the bags of baby gear that Gab had slowly begun to accumulate, it only took three trips to move everything. Too absorbed in exams to think about much else, the girls planned to purchase furniture after they'd moved in. They figured they'd survive using beanbags, camping mats and milk crates until then. Anders had brought camping mats for them to sleep on, as instructed by his second-eldest daughter. But when he saw Gab, he decided that a camping mat would not do for a young lady seven-months-pregnant.

"Off we go!" he said, with theatrical flair. "No sleeping mats. We are off to buy some new beds!" Gab protested, especially when it became clear that Anders planned to pay for her new bed as well as for Freya's, but he wasn't having a bar of it. His charm and nonchalant generosity gradually overcame Gab's embarrassment, and by the evening, two flat-packed bedframes and two vac-packed mattresses had transformed into spaces of welcome comfort, one in each bedroom.

As that busy day drew to a close, sushi was ordered for dinner. The four girls and Anders sat around the loungeroom—on the floor, on beanbags, on boxes—eating and chatting in tired satisfaction. Afterwards, Gab and Freya hugged and thanked their support crew with much gratitude.

Tomorrow, Gab would put together the baby's cot—a no-fuss, minimalist affair. Whereas all the baby stuff had been squeezed and shoved in her old room, here she would set it up neatly, folding baby clothes into a new set of drawers and neatly packing nappies, wipes, and clothes the next two sizes up into the wardrobe. She would decorate the apartment with her indoor plants and Freya would add her collection of paintings and sculptures; then, they would pore over listings of second-hand couches and tables and bookshelves.

It was already beginning to feel like home.

CHAPTER 55

January

"Freya! Freya!"

Freya heard the fearful cries before she'd even opened the front door. The panic in Gab's voice gripped her. Freya dropped her keys and her purse, everything clattering to the floor, and rushed into the lounge room to find Gab on all fours on the rug.

"What is it Gab? What's wrong?" she cried.

"I don't know!" wailed Gab, "Am I in labour?"

"I don't know, are you?" asked Freya. "I mean, have you had pain during the day?"

"Yes ... a little bit ... but I thought it was just cramps. It felt like ... OWWWWWW!" Gab stopped and howled. "Freyaaaaaa! I can't do this! Help me!"

Freya put a hand gently on Gab's shoulder. She'd grown up with a GP for a mother. She knew all about natural, biological processes. Still, real life labour—if this was what it was—was very different from the idea of it.

"Breathe, Gab," encouraged Freya, reverting to the one tip guaranteed to be relevant. "You can do this. Breathe, just breeeaaaathe."

The contraction continued, but Gab softened slightly at the waist.

"Remember what they said in birthing classes," Freya reminded Gab, gradually getting herself together. She had accompanied Gab to a number of birthing classes at the hospital. "Remember, this pain is good pain. Your body knows what it's doing. Breathe it out."

And then everything was normal again.

"I'm okay. I'm okay," said Gab. "But Freya—what do we do now?"

"I'm going to call Mum," said Freya. "Remember, they said not to come to hospital too early. First labours can take a long time."

"A long time!" cried Gab. She'd known this fact without really comprehending it until now. "I can't do this, Freya! I can't!" and the overwhelm crashed over and through her, drawing her into a vortex more abstract than the contractions, but no less real.

"You *can* do this Gab," said Freya. "You're the strongest person I know."

Gab got up from all fours on the floor and tried to lay on her side on the couch instead; she pulled out her phone to distract herself with a game, while Freya went to pick up her keys and purse and phone her mother. Within minutes, Gab's body tightened again, her eyes took on the look of complete focus, and a cry of pain echoed through the house. Gab's lips were stretched in a grimace, teeth bared as she tried to breath through it; those lips had always worked so hard to guard and hide the impulses that lay behind them until recent months.

Freya had never seen anyone in pain like this before. Was it really necessary for a process so common, so ubiquitous, so essential, to be so brutal? She was dying to know why Gab had not phoned her earlier, how she could *possibly* have gotten to this point without saying anything—without realising. Freya had an unarticulated sense that perhaps Gab hadn't wanted to realise it. And she didn't blame her.

The rest of Freya's family were staying in Ocean Grove for a fortnight of their summer holidays. Freya had opted to stay with Gab, but the two girls had driven down to hang out with Freya's family a few times, with increasing trepidation as Gab's due date drew nearer and nearer.

CHAPTER 56

"Mum?"

Saanvi answered the phone after a couple of rings.

"Hi Freya, how are you?"

"Mum, I think Gab's in labour."

"Okay." There was a subtle switch in Saanvi's tone. "Where is she? Is she alright?"

"We're at home. We're just in the lounge room. But the contractions seem really strong!"

"Can you put me on speakerphone, dear?"

"Sure." Freya did so.

"Girls, can you hear me?"

"Yes," they replied.

"Have your waters broken, Gab?" she asked.

"I don't know!" replied Gab. "How would I know?"

"Some women feel a sudden pop or a gushing of water, but with others, it is more gradual—a continuous leak. The baby might feel lower inside you."

Gab shook her head.

"No, Mum," said Freya, "Gab's waters haven't broken."

"Okay," said Saanvi. "How long between contractions?"

"I don't know," said Freya, "Not long. Gab?" But Gab's eyes were shut and she breathing in through her nose and out through her mouth like she never had before. The presence of Saanvi's voice added a degree of stability at least.

"Mum, Gab's having another contraction. It can't have been long since the last one ... maybe three minutes? Or five?"

"Okay, make sure to time between them, from the start of one contraction to the beginning of the next," instructed Saanvi. "In the meantime, is Gab comfortable?"

"NO!" squawked Gab, as the contraction eased. "But that's just the contractions," she said, as she found her breath again. "That was a really short one."

"It sounds like they're a still a little unpredictable," said Saanvi. "That can happen, especially when it's your first labour. It's happening quickly enough though, so just find a comfortable position for your contractions—whatever feels natural. Use towels or cushions if you need. You can even take a shower. The warm water will help."

"But Mum! Don't we need to get to hospital?" asked Freya.

"Maybe," said Saanvi. "But if it's too early, they'll just send you home. Gab, when did your contractions start?"

"I don't know," confessed Gab. "I started feeling pain this morning, maybe about nine o'clock? But it wasn't much. I just thought it was cramping."

"Okay. Well, it's nothing like the movies," assured Saanvi. "It often takes a long time, at least with first babies. Your body needs to warm up. The more you can relax and be comfortable, the smoother the process will be. You can call your hospital midwife at any time. In fact, you should do that now so they know to expect you. They will tell you when to come in."

Saanvi's calmness and her normalisation of the situation reduced Gab's panic. It was all happening, but not all at once. There was time.

"Okay, so I should call the hospital?"

"Yes, do that."

Gab did so from her own phone, notwithstanding another contraction which came a good seven minutes after the last. It was all routine for the midwife on the phone, who instructed Gab to come in either when her waters broke or when her contractions were consistently four minutes apart.

"Gab!" cried Freya suddenly, "how are you getting to the hospital?"

Neither had a car. It was one and a half kilometres from their apartment to the hospital.

"I don't know … I'll walk I guess," said Gab.

"WHAT?" cried usually-unflappable Freya. "You can't walk to hospital in labour, Gab!"

"It's probably better than riding my bike," joked Gab wryly. "Or taking a tram!" Getting on the trams during pregnancy had felt risky enough with all their violent stopping and starting; in labour it was unthinkable.

"Walking is very good for labour," Saanvi interjected calmly. "So it will be fine if Gab feels comfortable to do so. It just depends on when you need to go there, Gab."

"What about *an ambulance*?!" exclaimed Freya.

"Not calling an ambulance," said Gab determinedly. She hated the thought of drama.

"Why?" asked Freya in disbelief.

"Just because, okay? Trust me." Gab was adamant.

"Sorry. A taxi then?"

Gab paused, closed her eyes and shut out the world for ninety seconds before they resumed their conversation.

"Freya, imagine if my waters broke in the cab! No way." Gab was mortified at the idea of being in such close quarters with a random taxi-driver at such a time. Her self-consciousness was so ingrained that it exerted power even then, in the most primal experience of her life. On the surface, this didn't make much sense, because there would be plenty of people on the streets if she walked. But at least this way, Gab had fresh air and space, and there were corners to hide in. She wouldn't be trapped. She'd be in control. Sort of.

"Your waters might break in the street!" exclaimed Freya, trying to temper her disbelief. "What if the pain is too intense and you can't walk? What if you give birth on the footpath?? It's not like you'd be in an ambulance for long ... or a taxi," she added, seeing Gab's face.

"Freya," Saanvi's tone carried a subtle warning.

"I'm just worried for you, Gab," Freya explained.

"It's okay," Gab said to her friend.

"Gab, if you want to walk, dear, you walk," said Saanvi staunchly. "If that is what your body is telling you to do, you do it. Freya will go with you. If it gets too much, you must call an ambulance, okay? Likewise, if you need to get to hospital in the middle of the night. If the contractions feel like they're continuous, without a break and getting stronger, your baby is close. Keep that in mind too, dear. But for now, I think you're still in the first stages of labour."

"First stage?" exclaimed Gab. "Saanvi, how long is this going to take?"

"Hard to say. The first stage is the longest," said Saanvi calmly. "Your body knows what to do. You can trust it. Just breathe, try to relax and go with it. Freya, can you carry Gab's bag for her when you walk to the hospital?"

"Yes, Mum, of course!" exclaimed Freya, still bamboozled at the idea of calmly walking through the city with her friend in the process of giving birth. But at least it wasn't far. Twenty minutes. Freya was sure they could get there in twenty minutes, even with having to stop for contractions.

CHAPTER 57

And so, three hours later, Gab walked. By seven o'clock in the evening, the contractions were coming faster, lasting longer, no more than four minutes apart. Saanvi had stayed on speaker phone the whole time.

Gab called the hospital to let them know they were coming. And then Freya shouldered Gab's backpack, labour-plan stuffed right at the top, and took Gab's arm.

"Are you sure, Gab?"

"It's fine," said Gab. She just wanted to walk. "Between the contractions, I'm fine." And she would be very good at hiding her pain from strangers.

Step-step-step-step-step. Pause. Breathe. Hold onto Freya. Wait. Step-step-step-step-step. One step at a time and she was getting closer. Each step, a step closer to motherhood, to her baby. It wasn't busy, but there were enough people about. Strangers stopped to ask Freya if her friend was alright when they saw her double over. The young ones were entirely shocked, panicked when Freya said that Gab was on her way to hospital to have a baby. Some of the older passersby were more knowing; three women who were out together for dinner decided to accompany the girls to the hospital to make sure they arrived safely. They buffered Gab and Freya as they walked on, with words of encouragement and gentle confidence in Gab.

And finally, Freya and the three women and Gab made it to the maternity ward of the hospital. Contractions were barely three minutes apart now; walking had sped things up. But Gab still had the presence of mind to ask Freya to take the three shepherding women's phone numbers, so that they could be given baby news.

They had made it this far. Gab was in safe hands now.

CHAPTER 58

Intense feelings emanated from a place within Gab she hadn't known existed. Deep within her abdomen, they moved downwards, outwards—deepening with every moment, pulling in the entirety of her being, her mind, her self.

Lying in the exam room, the midwife checked the degree of Gab's cervical dilation—an uncomfortable procedure that Gab got through with sheer grit. It was time to get to a birthing suite—and to hustle. Gab's waters hadn't yet broken, but they soon would.

Freya had been standing outside the exam room while the midwife checked Gab, but when the midwife asked Gab if she had anyone to support her, she called out to her friend. Freya came in, helped Gab up off the exam table and stepped into a role that she had never imagined would be part of her university experience. She was ready to grow into the space that the role demanded of her.

With Freya supporting one arm, the midwife the other, Gab walked, very slowly now, to the nearest birthing suite. There were no gaps between contractions anymore. The girls had arrived just in time.

In the birthing suite, Gab didn't want to lie down. She needed to be on her hands and knees; she knew it deeply. Her focus was complete; that transition between cervical opening and the beginning passage of the baby out towards the world was one of entire intuition. She had to go with her body; to trust that she knew more than she knew. She also had to trust that the unbearable pain wouldn't be the death of her. This was such an acute synchrony of opposites—surrender and agency, relinquishment and gain, letting go and being caught up—*being* the process itself.

The pain moved from a deep, gruelling push in the pit of her abdomen—when waters finally broke with a sudden burst of impact—to that intense burning pain that heralded the beginning of birth.

"I can't do it!" Gab cried, in alarmed desperation.

"You're nearly there," said Felicity, a young, strong midwife. "You *can* do this. We know you can. Now, just rest for a moment; don't push yet. We don't want any tearing. The urge to push will come again in a moment, but I just want you to breathe, take it slow. I'll tell you when."

Freya was by Gab's head and shoulders; Gab leaning on her own elbow's, squeezing Freya's hand like her life depended on it. The midwife sent affirming nods to Freya too:

"That's it, hold her hands. Gab, you're doing great."

And then, the pain rose, and rose and rose and at that moment when it couldn't possibly get any worse and Gab felt she was about to explode or disintegrate, there was a sudden *whoosh* of release.

"Your baby's head is out!" cried Felicity warmly. "Oh, well done, Gab! Now, there'll be one more big push in a moment, and … "

Suddenly Gab was crying and Freya was crying and a new little, tiny voice was crying too.

There he was.

A little boy.

Felicity helped Gab roll over and pull off her shirt, and she laid this little, tiny boy on Gab's naked chest; Gab didn't care that she was naked because she was all new too.

The strange opposite feelings that had run through Gab for months and years suddenly weren't parallel anymore—not in that moment. They became intwined in an explosion of warmth when

Gab looked down at her son. Her *real son*. Smooth and tender, with the finest blonde hairs and already gingery little eyebrows. He was the most beautiful thing Gab had ever seen.

That is not to say that in the next moment, Gab didn't look at the little pink lump in her arms and wonder what the heck to do with it and how this could possibly, possibly be true. She was galled by the overwhelming residual pain of her body, the after-pains of labour; her uterus contracted to half its size in an absurdly short time—wasn't the pain meant to be over after birth? It certainly wasn't. And she struggled too with helping her baby latch on to feed, because both were learning and it was strange, even if natural. These were things no one had told Gab to expect. It was as much a learning curve for her as for her baby.

But there was also wonder and delight—and newness, so much newness. The midwives allowed Freya to stay in hospital overnight with Gab, and she warmed Gab's heat-pack countless times, propped up her pillows, helped Gab to the bathroom, and held the tiny, warm little bundle when Gab was desperate for sleep.

This was a beginning. This was Gab's *own* family, to be more than what her own had been. And she took into it all she had learned, and all the ways in which she had been hurt, and a passion to do everything in her power to be different, *not* to repeat the cycle, not to pass on that emptiness, those gaps, that indignity, to her child. She didn't know how she was going to manage this, but she was going to manage it.

This was tenacity.

CHAPTER 59

January

River James Anthony Lander had arrived. Gab was a mother. Gab and her baby spent two nights in hospital and afterwards, she did *not* walk herself home; her pelvic floor was too gutted for that. Freya had to bring the baby-capsule to the hospital before Gab could put it into the taxi to take them fifteen hundred meters home again. The three ladies who had shepherded the girls to hospital along the city streets were delighted to hear of River's safe arrival. They sent Gab flowers.

Saanvi organised a very practical gift bag for Gab, with packs and packs of super-sized pads, a heat bag and Panadol, breast pads for leakages, and lots and lots of snacks. She brought it around with two bags of frozen meals on the first day home, including some of her famous butter chicken curry. It was very helpful to have a conscientious Mum to borrow, Gab thought.

Midwives visited Gab and River frequently during their first week, too. Gab's milk came in painfully with absurd jet-stream let-downs, and her body was something changed and different. There were hours and hours of feeding, sometimes with many frustrating, failed attempts to latch a fussing baby on in the dark. There were night-wakings and daytime naps. Freya however, was relaxed about River's presence in the apartment. She held him while Gab ate breakfast, took him for walks so that Gab could have a shower, and usually slept through his night-wakings. It was hard for Freya to see her friend in tears some days, exhausted and foggy; she felt out of her depth and tired some days too, but she wasn't scared off.

River had a distinct presence. Things were different. He wasn't very noisy yet; feed him, cuddle him, and he was happy—so Gab did, while reading up profusely on parenting styles, developmental milestones and the norms of baby rearing in different cultures. Brian brought 'Uncle Jack' to visit when River was one week old. And Tony brought Gina to visit a week later, playing the role of supervisor and Gab's backup, which he did well. Gab had phoned Tony the day after River's birth; Tony had indeed heard from Gina about Gab's pregnancy but hadn't wanted to intrude and, like Gab, hadn't known what to say. But he'd been waiting on tenterhooks with growing anxiety as Gab's due date approached, and was delighted and relieved to hear of River's safe arrival and Gab's good health. The strength of these feelings surprised him.

Gina was besotted when she met her grandson despite everything—though of course, she came with plenty of advice she was unqualified to give. But it was all Gab could do to take her son back out of Gina's arms again when Tony declared it was time for them to leave—not before he surreptitiously stuffed $200 into Gab's hand. James and Melinda had a gift pack sent to Gab. She phoned to say thanks and ended up regaling Mr. C. with her labour story; it was so fresh in her experience and so much in need of processing.

The timing of River's birth was serendipitous and Gab was glad that at least in that way she'd stumbled across some good luck. He was born in January, right in the middle of the uni summer break, and a couple of weeks after Gab's nineteenth birthday. Classes didn't start back until the beginning of March when River would be almost three months old.

Maybe River was relaxed or maybe empathic Gab was attuned to his signals and was quickly responsive. She had an instinctual drive to nurture; the foundation must have been laid by the sensitive care of her grandmother in her first years of life, compounded by the years of attending to Jack and craving what she herself lacked.

Jack was besotted with River and constantly pestered Brian to drive him down to visit. Then Brian invited Gab to come and stay with them for the first weekend of each month. When Gab told Tony about it, he promised to drive down to pick them up, ferrying them to Brian's each time. He just wanted to see them both, and Jack.

Before River was six weeks old, the health nurse had encouraged Gab to join the mother's group at the local Health Centre. But Gab was reticent to join. She feared the humiliation of being the youngest in the group; she also feared questions about her relational status or about the identity of River's father. *That* she wanted to keep right to herself.

CHAPTER 60

Two weeks before classes began, Gab received an unexpected phone call.

"Hello?" she answered an unknown caller, while sitting on the couch juggling River on her lap.

"Hi, is that Gabrielle?" a female voice came down the line.

"Yes. Who's this?"

"Tory. Robbie Walker's girlfriend." Gab dropped the phone. She picked it up. Her life flashed before her eyes. "Didn't you used to live with Steph?" asked Tory acerbically.

"Yeah, um, last year," said Gab, her heart racing as though she were being interrogated by the police for a suspected crime.

"Steph told me something interesting."

"What's that?"

"She said you had a baby."

"Yeah, I ... I did. I do."

"Well, Steph told me something else kind of interesting. She said that you and Robbie got *very close* at a party I wasn't at last year." Tory's voice peaked as her sentence ended, as though she were struggling to restrain hysteria. Gab's head spun; she was dizzy, she had to lie down. She didn't know what to say. She didn't know what to do.

"Is it true?" pressed Tory, whose tone was both menacing and fearful. "Tell me! Is it *true?* Is *Robbie* the father?"

"I don't know," said Gab. What else could she say?

"What the hell does *that* mean? How can you not know? What are you saying?!"

"I don't know how to answer."

"Robbie cheated on me last year, didn't he? With you!" Tory sounded defeated now and Gab's heart did a strange thing and leapt out towards Tory with painful compassion. She couldn't bring herself to lie straight out. She just couldn't, because in a weird way, Tory deserved to know. Gab tried to imagine herself in Tory's shoes. Wouldn't *she* want to know the truth, if her boyfriend had cheated on her? Gab gulped.

"Yes. He did. I'm so so … "

The phone went dead.

CHAPTER 61

Robbie wants to talk with you.

Steph's text message arrived the next morning. Gab ignored it, but a couple of hours later, Steph texted again.

You can't hide from him forever, Gab.

Gab was becoming frantic.

"Freya!" She blew into the kitchen with River on her hip, where Freya was making breakfast for herself.

"What do I do!?" Gab burst into tears as the rollercoaster of the last twelve months hit her like a steam train.

Freya came over and took River. Gab sat down on a stool at the bench with her head in her hands. Her stomach felt like the ocean in a hurricane and her eyes were blinded by sprays of torrential waves.

"What's wrong, Gab?" Freya asked seriously. Gab hadn't told her about Tory's call. She'd just hoped it was a once off and that everything would go away.

Gab tried to breathe, but she was panicky.

"Tory ... Robbie's girlfriend ..."

"Oh no."

"She called me ... and, and ... she somehow found out about the party ... and Steph messaged to say Robbie wants to ... talk with me. *What do I do, Freya?*"

"*Steph* messaged you? Why Steph?"

"I don't know. I mean ... I do ... Because it was Steph who told Tory! About me and Robbie ... " Gab stifled sobs.

"OH MY GOD! STEPH! I'm going to kill her!" cried Freya. "I mean, *how dare she*!" continued Freya. "This is none of her business. *None*!"

"Well, it was her party when ..."

"No! No, Gab. It's got nothing to do with her."

Gab hiccupped. River tried to eat Freya's hair.

"You're caught right in the middle of it, little man, aren't you?" Freya said to River, gradually detangling his chubby fingers from her hair.

"What's Robbie going to do, Freya? Will he take River?"

"No, Gab, he will not. That is not going to happen. I know it's hard not to race ahead to the worst possible scenario, but let's take it a step at a time. So, Robbie wants to talk to you."

Gab nodded.

"Okay, Gab. Talk to him. You're brave. You can handle it."

"I can't."

"You can."

"I just can't do it."

"Okay. That's fine Gab. But just remember—*you* did not cheat on Tory. Robbie did."

CHAPTER 62

Late February

First semester of Gab's second year at uni was starting in a week. Gab was spending all her time at home, failing to keep her mind off the whole spiralling situation. The phone had started ringing again and again with an unknown number, but whoever it was would never leave a message. Gina called too, asking about River and telling Gab that she feared her cold symptoms were really pneumonia. Gab wanted to disappear to where no one could find her and her baby, or bother them. Could she? Could she run away? Move countries? New Zealand sounded nice. After a week of Gab ignoring phone calls from the unknown number, the caller left a message one morning. It was Robbie.

"Hi, it's Robbie. Can you call me? Bye."

As if, Gab thought.

But he called again that day. And again. And by three o'clock in the afternoon he'd worn her down. When the phone rang, her thumb pressed 'answer', even as her brain was a screaming red siren: *NO! NO! NO!*

"Hello?"

"Gab? It's Robbie."

She was silent. Her whole universe rushed through her in that moment—mainly River—and she instinctively stood up, as though to protect him, while he gurgled happily on a mat on the floor.

"How did you get my number?" Gab asked.

"Steph."

"Oh. Um, what else did Steph tell you?" She didn't want to give away more than she had to.

"That you have a baby now."

"Oh yeah, I do," said Gab feebly. "He was born three months ago." She wished it would all end. Why did Robbie have to exist?

"Did you tell Tory about that party last year?"

"No."

"Who did?"

Should she rat on Steph? She was so eager not to be in trouble herself.

"Steph did." It slipped out.

"*Damn it*! Why?"

"I don't know. Ask Steph."

"So, you really have a baby?" he asked.

"Yes." She'd already told him that.

"I thought Tory was joking!"

"No. It's true," said Gab.

"But it's not ... I mean, I don't even know ... "

"It happened at Steph and Dylan's party," said Gab quietly, surprising herself. Whatever had happened to keeping Robbie out? Suddenly that intention was out the window, turfed out by the unruly, strange part of her that had just answered Robbie's call. It would have been *so* much easier to say it wasn't his and to leave it at that. But somehow, she *couldn't*. It was *his* responsibility too.

"You *think* it's mine? Don't play that game! It can't be mine! I don't even know what happened. Probably nothing!"

"Then why did you call? Something happened, Robbie. I have a baby now. And ... it has to be yours."

"I don't believe you."

"Okay."

"And don't you *dare* talk to my girlfriend again."

"Okay. But just so you know, she called *me*," retorted Gab. *If she's still your girlfriend*, she mentally added.

"I don't care. And don't come to me for support either, pretending it's my baby when it's not. I bet you've said that to all the guys you've slept with! You're a gold digger."

"NO," Gab almost screamed. "I'm not! I hadn't ever ... " She wanted to strangle the idiot; the hypocrisy made her livid.

And then, an entirely different feeling washed over her, as though the ghost of her missing father appeared before her in a flash.

"Don't ... you want to meet him?" she whispered.

"Who?"

"Your son."

Silence.

"Not unless you prove he's mine," said Robbie.

"Do you ... want me to prove it?" asked Gab.

"I don't know. Do you want to prove it?" he asked back, suddenly with the harsh edge worn off his voice so that it came as a genuine question.

"I don't know," replied Gab honestly.

"Okay then."

"Okay."

And Robbie hung up.

CHAPTER 63

Gab tried to focus on the future. Uni was starting in a couple of days. Robbie wasn't taking her baby. River had gained almost three kilos, was an experienced feeder and was becoming very interested in the world. Gab didn't really want to put him in childcare, not just yet; she missed him enough when Freya took him on a walk in the evening, even though Gab also craved the oxygen of space. So, while he was on the waiting list at two local childcare centres, her intention was to take him to class with her. Freya was busy with her own full-time study and her ushering job; besides, she already did so much help out and Gab didn't want to ask for more. So, why not take River along to class? It seemed as natural to bring him with her as it did to bring her backpack—notwithstanding the vast differences in nature between the two. Gab assumed others would see it that way too; what could be more important than looking after her child, and why should she miss out on her education because of it? River took up less room than her backpack, even if he was a little more distracting.

Lectures were posted online and could be accessed later, so Gab only had four contact hours a week of tutorials to manage. Anticipating this, she oscillated between feeling that it would be entirely impossible to juggle study and parenting—some days she could barely string a sentence together and couldn't be bothered eating much—and other days she couldn't wait to get back into learning. The reality of constant physical contact with her baby, of always being needed, raised Gab's hackles sometimes; it triggered her implicit recollections of how she had been trapped, buried under responsibility, throughout all her teenage years. At the same time, Gab loved River and couldn't imagine life without him. He was part of her. And he would be part of her study and her vocation.

Classes started and Gab became a pro at strapping fluffy-headed River onto her and carrying him around on her front or her back. The wrap in which River nestled was like a second womb. Gab even figured out how to feed River in there. Of course, sometimes she did take him out to feed him and the immature, inexperienced students around her would look at her with complete surprise, or disgust, or incredulity—as though she wasn't doing something that human beings had been doing since the beginning of time, something that ensured their survival. Gab had come a long way from the timid, responsible child who was afraid of rocking the boat, or of offending others in the slightest, or of exposing any part of her body to the outside world. Motherhood brought with it a tenacious drive to do the best for her baby, no matter who was around.

One of her two tutors didn't bat an eyelid when she brought River with her to class. Gab had emailed before the start of classes to half ask, half explain that she would be bringing her infant along. In fact, that one tutor was incredibly supportive, making sure Gab was comfortable, checking in with her to make sure she was coping with reading and assessment demands, making sure she knew she was free to talk with her about any concerns she might have. Gab's other tutor made her feel like her baby was an alien on a foreign planet, an intruder who didn't belong anywhere near a university campus—however, Gab's newfound obstinacy, her stubborn tenacity, tided her over. She mostly attended anyway. But she did miss four tutorials (which was the maximum she was allowed to miss and still pass the subject) because it wasn't particularly easy to sit there and feel alienated.

Some of the other students got behind her though, and by the end of semester, River had become something of a celebrity. Her peers gradually adjusted to the idea of her breastfeeding in class (Freya rolled her eyes when Gab told her about their initial reactions), and many would stop Gab to say hi and baby-talk with River. A couple of other students even offered to hold him in class while Gab finished off written exercises, especially on those days when he was extra fussy or didn't want to sit in the pram. As the initial walls of nervous unfamiliarity were worn down, Gab's classmates became a community that was part of her journey, buoying her up and carrying her along—even if that one tutor continued to be obstinately aloof and a few students stayed persistently disengaged and ignored them both.

CHAPTER 64

But what was Gab going to do about Robbie? Their discussion dogged her. It was like she was living two lives—the happy student Gab who enjoyed her classes, who others got to know as part of their learning community, who thrived with the academic challenges in front of her, and who juggled her study and parenting responsibilities with dexterity and intelligence. Then there was the anxious Gab, the tumultuous Gab, the one who she became when she was awake in the night, feeding her baby, surrounded by shadows and haunting sounds in the dark. She was the Gab who bore the scars of Gina's persistent dependence, which hadn't relented even now, even if they had something new and positive to talk about—River—as they never had before. This Gab was being drawn down, down, into an ever tighter, deeper spiral, tormented by the thought of Tory, of Steph, of Robbie; torn by the desire for Robbie to *care*, to see what an amazing little person his son was, how adorable, how sweet—yet with a deep, bitter resentment at having to carry the entire load of responsibility alone ... again ...

And then again, she felt inclined to make the most of Robbie's words—that he didn't want to hear from her unless she could prove that River was his. This was her out. This was what she wanted. If she never proved it, she'd never have to talk with Robbie again, presumably. But then there was River—was he missing out if she didn't 'prove it' to Robbie, like Melinda had said he would? Could she honestly tell her son now that his father was ignorant of his existence, as she'd planned to? She didn't know and it was unravelling her. It was too much to figure out. She was not equal to it.

After exams were over, that anxious Gab was looming larger and larger. She crashed. She didn't even want to leave the house unless she had to anymore, and it was all the more inviting to stay home because she now had an active, wriggly, noisy six-month-old for whom any journey out into the world meant utter preparedness, lots of energy and many layers of stress. It was easier to stay home, to avoid it all, to block the world out. Only in blocking the world out, she locked herself into her own mind-world, and it became bigger and bigger until it was engulfing her. The next semester of uni seemed a million miles away—a faint and hazy dream that might not even come.

"Gab," said Freya one day after dinner, sitting down on the couch next to her, while River crawled back and forth along the lounge room floor after a jingly ball, "I'm worried about you."

Tears spilled down Gab's cheeks and Freya hugged her.

"I know looking after a baby is really, really hard. And you're doing an amazing job," encouraged Freya.

"But?" sniffed Gab. "I hear a *but* coming."

"No 'but' is coming," smiled Freya. "I think you're doing an amazing job *and* I'm worried about you. You seem ... I don't know ... "

"Tired?" asked Gab. "Stressed? But isn't that normal? Besides, I went to class, I finished exams, I managed all of semester with a baby." Gab's tone was flat, empty; she couldn't even quite manage defensiveness.

"I know you did. And it's stunning. But now you seem so sad, Gab!"

Gab began shaking with sobs.

"I am and I don't know why!"

"Do you think it might be a good idea to ask for help?" Freya suggested gently.

"From who?" Gab sniffed.

"Well, the doctor. Maybe a psychologist."

"I don't need a doctor!" exclaimed Gab. "And definitely not a psychologist!"

Freya didn't think it would be kind to remind Gab of the last time she'd said that, and she was wise enough not to press the point.

"Okay, no worries," said Freya, getting up. "I'm going to get ready for bed." She turned to River. "Goodnight sweetie-kins!" she said, bending down and giving him a kiss on his warm, soft baby head.

Gab lay in bed that night thinking about what Freya had said ... and wanting to die. She just couldn't keep going under this load. It was too much. This was the end. She looked at the silhouette of her baby in the dark, lying in his cot and sleeping sweetly. She wanted to give up, stop trying ... but she couldn't. She was trapped. Who would look after her baby if she quit? She *did* still care about that, even if she didn't care about anything else. Gab thought of her hard life with her mother. She thought of all that she had yearned for. Then she imagined her own son missing out on those things too— on the love, warmth and kindness that she wanted to give him, as his mum.

If she was going to keep going—for him—she needed something. All the stuff with Robbie, with her mum, parenting—it was too much to figure out on her own. Her impulse when she was younger had always been to resist help, because she knew that support could dissolve when you least expected it ... and then you'd fall. And it would really hurt. More sad, more hurt, more disappointed than when you started. Falling. Injured. Better to only rely on yourself.

But how could she keep going alone? She didn't want anyone else's help, and she didn't want to admit that things were hard. But she knew she couldn't keep doing things in this way, with the anxious Gab hiding curled up inside her, only to unfurl and encase her every night as her heart raced and thoughts of Robbie and Tory and

Steph and her mother—not to mention feelings of her own worthlessness and failures and inadequacies—swallowed her up into a dark and endless abyss from which she could never climb out, and which felt hopeless, engulfing, final.

She looked again at River and she felt angry. It was all *his* fault; his, for coming into existence against so many odds! The rage coursed through her like a shock and she squeezed her pillow around her head. It wasn't the first time; and of course she was angry—how was it possible for her not to be? She had endured years of subjugation, years of suppressed fury at her mother, stored up for everything unreasonable, unfair and illogical. She had been angry all along and she'd had no idea—for everything Gina had forced Gab to endure, every burden she had left her to carry. But as a child, she could never have taken that anger out on her mother, because she was still dependent on her. She didn't have any other family to go to. What would have happened to her and Jack if things at home disintegrated?

But Gab was the one in control now. She wasn't the small one anymore. She was the one in charge here; her baby was the needy one. Why did he need her so much? She shook with rage. Even though he was so soft and small, he was controlling her life, directing it in ways she never imagined it would go. She was angry at him for that, and for what it said about her—that she, a competent human who could carry more than others her age, who brought up her little brother and who withstood all the barrages of Gina's turbulence, was being undone by this tiny little fragment of a human being. It was like red rain pouring in her mind. Then she sat up and gripped her head, paralysed by the sheer intensity of her own rage and simultaneously by the deluge of guilt and disgrace that came with it.

How *could* she feel such awful things about her baby? It *wasn't* his fault. That was entirely illogical. He needed her protection, her help. She thought of what it would mean to mistreat him; she imagined what it would be like. What was wrong with her? How could she even think this way? She felt she did not deserve to exist. Always this guilt like a deadly shadow following her, even pushing in front of her as if anticipating her next move; she could not escape it because she could not escape herself. She should curl up in a ball and hide and never come out ever again. She didn't want anyone to see her.

And then in her mind, an image flashed as vivid as the day. Gina, in her sunroom. Gina, who never wanted adventure. Gina, for whom life was too much, who had hidden herself away and taken out her frustration on her children. Gab knew that she did *not* want to be like her mother. That struck. She would *not* be like Gina.

But ... what if it was predetermined? What if fate was stronger than free will and Gab couldn't help but follow in her mother's footsteps? Gina always seemed powerless at the hands of destiny. What if Gab really was too? Then she was frightened, terrified. That fear, mingled with ripples of horrified guilt emanating from her anger, was more powerful in that moment even than the desire to love and nurture her child. Gab was afraid, deathly afraid and tormented.

Alone in the night, in that moment, there was one tiny flicker of light. It was a small flicker, a long way off, but it was there. Gab thought back to what Saanvi had said the first time they had met, at the doctors' surgery. Gab had been terrified that Saanvi would diagnosed her with depression, like her mother. *There are genetic factors involved ...* Saanvi had said ... *but there's generally a lot more to it than that.* In other words, there was hope.

It was a very thin thread to hold onto, but it was there.

CHAPTER 66

The next morning Gab went and knocked on Freya's bedroom door.

"I'll go to the doctor," she said quietly, and that was all. She didn't say why and she hid her anger exceptionally well, which perhaps was part of the reason it was so frighteningly strong within her. She walked off again to give River his breakfast, because he had started on solid foods now and loved his mashed banana.

And Freya felt relieved because she didn't know where all this was heading, and it felt like more than she could manage or help with. After exams had finished, she had sensed Gab's ongoing frustration in the way she moved, in how she slammed the fridge shut, in the sharp edge that snuck into her tone. She noticed how quickly Gab became deflated when things became difficult, how sensitive she was, and how quick to read River's baby responses as her own failure. It wasn't like that all the time; there were laughs and fun too. There was joy at having made it through the first semester of uni with River by her side; but Freya had noticed a distinct turbulence and figured that the more points of stability that Gab could connect with, the better.

* * *

Gab visited a doctor near their home this time, instead of visiting Saanvi. She and Saanvi had decided after discussion that it was easiest this way; Gab could simply relate to Saanvi as Freya's Mum now, rather than as *doctor*. Gab was nervous going to a new clinic, but much less frightened than the first time the year before. Nine months of appointments, friendly midwives, and a positive experience in the maternity ward had begun to lessen her fear.

She didn't tell the doctor too much, but it was enough for the doctor to see that extra support for this young, single mother with a six-month-old infant could only be a good thing. The doctor suggested medication to help Gab manage her anxiety and stabilise her mood, and then wrote up a care plan for her to see a psychologist—who, the doctor assured her, would not mind if she took River along.

The medication was Gab's secret, another source of shame—because of course, she was reminding herself of her mother. So she didn't tell Freya—until the side effects felt so awful after the first few days that she begged her friend to take River so she could go to bed with a headache and the strangest feeling of muted mental tumult that she had ever experienced.

I'm morphing into my mother, she thought numbly as she lay there hiding under the covers. *I can't do it. I can't.* The thought of getting out of the house, going to talk with someone for an hour while River fussed and wriggled, and that someone being a *psychologist* ... it was too much.

CHAPTER 67

"Tell me why you're here," said Taz, the short-spiky-haired, khaki-shirted psychologist. It was the first question she asked on Gab's first visit. Gab's fear of turning out like her mother and her disinclination for letting people down had trumped her overwhelming inertia when it came to getting out of the house and down to her appointment.

She and Taz sat outside in a small garden with a sandpit and a reflective labyrinth and bees buzzing around lavender bushes that reminded Gab bittersweetly of Tony's place. Gab had laid River down on a mat on the grass and he was happily banging and whacking the toys she had brought him, shuffling this way and that, tugging at the grass and tasting it. He was a welcome focus-point for Gab. It was much easier to talk to Taz while looking down at River—using him as a decoy, handing him toys, averting too much ingestion of grass—instead of looking Taz in the face.

Gab didn't know how to answer Taz's question at first. But she eventually said, "Because I don't want to turn out like my mother." And that was just the sort of answer Taz could work with, because then she could ask, "Why's that?" and add, "Tell me about your mother?"

"Ha, she's crazy," answered Gab.

"And what does that mean?" smiled Taz, hoping Gab would uncover some of the hidden fears and labels she unconsciously held over herself and her mother at the same time.

That first session was not easy and Gab was exhausted for a week afterwards—on top of the standard exhaustion that comes with keeping a six month old occupied and alive. Just as she was picking herself up after the first appointment, the next session came around, and then the next; Taz had suggested they meet weekly at first.

During their fourth session, Gab told Taz about Robbie. Taz hadn't asked about River's father; she gave Gab space to share in her own words and way. Gab told Taz all about the party and about the conversation with her mother that had precipitated her desire to forget everything, to let it all go. She told Taz about finding her jeans scrunched up near her head after she'd woken with Robbie's arm draped over her—of seeing him in his boxer shorts, and of the haunting gap—not knowing what had really happened.

Gab cried when she told Taz what it was like to find out she was pregnant, of sitting in the university toilet block alone and weeing on those sticks, twice. She thought she hadn't wanted Robbie to know, she said. It had seemed too complicated. But what if she was turning out like her mother, who had barred any interaction with her own father? What did her son need? And what if Robbie didn't want him? Or, what if Robbie wanted him too much? River was all hers now. Did she want to share him with someone she didn't even know?

Steph's betrayal and Tory's phone call were weighing heavily, pinning her down in a spiral of tumult. As she recounted Tory's phone call to Taz, she felt she was talking about someone else, not herself. The person who had done the things that Tory accused her of—who had fallen pregnant in the way she had—*wasn't* her and she *couldn't* accept it. She did *not* go to parties and get drunk and sleep with strangers who already had girlfriends. That was not her. And if it was, just who the hell was she anyway? And then Taz asked, *Who was judging her? What was wrong with being a person like that?* But Gab didn't *want* to be a person 'like that' because that was the kind of person who hurt other people, who did stupid things, who ruined other people's lives. And Taz said it was okay to make mistakes, and that the very fact that Gab didn't *want* to hurt other people meant by default that she was *not* the person she was afraid she was.

"And maybe," added Taz during that fourth session, "the girl who went to the party and got drunk and slept with Robbie was carrying more than she realised; maybe she was the girl who had endured years of emotional abuse and neglect at the hands of her mother—the sort of abuse that was so difficult to see, so impossible to quantify or even verify—and who had finally become fed up with carrying someone else's pain."

Gab didn't want to realise that she was that girl. Because what did that mean? It meant she was vulnerable and soft; she had been hurt, deeply, crucially, perhaps irreparably. It wasn't fair. She wasn't that strong, invincible character who could deal with anything, and maybe everyone else had seen that except her. How heinously embarrassing. To recognise this meant pain, recognition of inadequacy and blind spots. If that pain got out, it would engulf her. She would drown; it was too much. She had caught fleeting glimpses of yearning, starving pain before, she told Taz—when she had watched Mr. C. with his kids; when she had spent time with Saanvi and Anders, seeing how they interacted with, respected and supported their girls, even at times with Tony. She had seen, in poignant, bloody brilliance, what she had completely missed out on. Home. Being invited into the families of others had given her the most painful and precious experiences of her life. And this had also given her a picture of the kind of mother she wanted to be for River, she told Taz.

And Taz said it was okay to be that vulnerable girl who had been hurt, and that the feelings would come and engulf her, but they would also do what feelings always do—subside and change as she allowed herself to feel them, to recognise them, to accept them as part of her story. She didn't have to be afraid of them.

And when Gab began to recognise this, the purposefulness that had pulsed through her as she thought of giving River all she had missed became more real, more enduring. She had always been aspirational, but the aspiration was becoming concrete self-belief. The loss of those guarded, defensive illusions of invincibility, in the past so seemingly necessary for survival, was the beginnings of hope and self-knowledge. This loss was more powerful than rage; or perhaps, it was the next incarnation of that rage. Gab had told Taz a bit about her fury, though she hadn't told Taz that it was River who often evoked it. But Taz was not in the least shocked or surprised by Gab's anger, and that helped. Taz knew how gruelling parenting could be.

At the end of her fourth session, Gab felt like she had scaled a mountain. She felt exhausted and out-of-breath, but somehow exhilarated, as if having gained a breath-taking new view. When the session concluded, Gab bundled River up, extracted the remaining grass from his hands (to his displeasure), collected his toys, blanket and baby-wipes, and juggled them all. Then, she wished she had a third arm as she tried to pay Taz for the session.

Taz helped Gab pack the pram. Then she looked at her.

"Gab," she said, "You are doing great."

Gab shrugged it off, but as she thought about it on the walk home, she realised that the voices in her life now—the ones she listened to most—were the ones who believed in her. She'd lived in the past with a voice that always dragged her down, and it had taken up residence in her own mind, filtering her interpretations of herself and her world. In trying to protect herself from it while living with it, she had inadvertently cut herself off from many good voices as well. She'd had to prop herself up alone—until now. Now she was really *hearing* those good voices, and she wanted to trust them. Dare she?

Gab pushed the pram along the footpath, now in the shade, now in the sun, now in the dappled light of their interplay. Could she do this? Could she make a real life for herself and her son? She didn't know. But she *couldn't* know unless she tried.

River gurgled with delight as Gab pointed out a dove dancing in a bird-bath. She suddenly felt thirsty to grow and learn; to push herself again. And that reminded her—she had just borrowed a new book on farmed micro-algae, a promising a source of sustainable non-animal protein for human consumption. Yes. She couldn't wait to get home and start reading it.

* * *

And this may not seem a very victorious, triumphant or auspicious place to leave Gab and River—after four of six sessions with a local psychologist somewhere in Melbourne, thinking about micro-algae farms in the mid-year uni break, halfway through a Bachelor of Agriculture and six months into parenting—but actually, it is. Because, as Taz pointed out to Gab, the ability to reach out and ask for help, the fact that Gab had stepped out with courage to make change, the fact that she had divulged some of her deepest fears in order to move beyond them, and the fact that she had made decisions that made sense and benefitted her—even though they went against her ingrained habits—were the sorts of wins that were the substance of a hopeful future. They were signs of mature fragility and burgeoning courage.

Gab had made up her mind and was making the best life possible for herself and her son. At the point where life looked as though it was disintegrating, where Gab had loosened her grip on herself and started to come apart at the seams—this was crucial to forward movement. One foot in front of the other, one minute after the next—that was what it would take. The challenges were great and the stakes were high; but Gab's courage and aspiration rose in step to meet them, within a constellation of support and encouragement that didn't fix anything, but made life meaningful.

This was Gab.

She was tenacity.

Hi there!
I hope you enjoyed *She, Tenacity*. 50% of proceeds from eBook and print book sales are being donated to *The Babes Project*, a wonderful organisation that supports and empowers women throughout pregnancy and early parenting. Find out more at https://thebabesproject.com.au
From, Sarah ☺

ABOUT THE AUTHOR:

Sarah Bacaller is a writer, researcher and audiobook producer from Melbourne, Australia. She is writing a PhD in philosophy, works part-time as a gardener and co-directs of *Voices of Today*, an audiobook production company (www.voicesoftoday.org). Sarah has narrated 40+ titles on Audible, including her novella, *The Fault Lines Founding Liberty*. She enjoys living on the urban-rural fringe in Boonwurrung/Bunurong country with her family.

To find out more, visit www.sarahbacaller.com

ACKNOWLEDGEMENTS

With heartfelt thanks to my generous test-readers:
Rach, AB, Becca, Cristina, Kate, Helen.